Where she found a manila folder.

She slipped it out, opened it directly beneath the lightbulb.

There were papers inside. A couple of sheets of thin unlined paper on which somebody had scribbled words. The handwriting was shaky, spidery, consisting of uneven loops and hastily joined letters, as if the writer had been working in a fury.

Christy narrowed her eyes. But it was so hard to make anything of the scrawls that coursed across the paper.

dear . . . when I . . . unhappy . . .
that last time . . . things going so wrong . . .
killing me . . . I don't see how I can
get out of this alive . . .

Thomas Altman

Dark Places

CORGI BOOKS

DARK PLACES

A CORGI BOOK 0 552 12696 9

First publication in Great Britain

PRINTING HISTORY
Corgi edition published 1985

Corgi Books are published by Transworld Publishers Ltd.,
Century House, 61-63 Uxbridge Road, Ealing, London W5 5SA,
in Australia by Transworld Publishers (Aust.) Pty. Ltd.,
26 Harley Crescent, Condell Park, NSW 2200, and in New
Zealand by Transworld Publishers (N.Z.) Ltd., Cnr. Moselle
and Waipareira Avenues, Henderson, Auckland.

Made and printed in Great Britain by
Hunt Barnard Printing Ltd., Aylesbury, Bucks.

To Rebecca, the second time around.

1

Christy sipped her drink. The party had been given to celebrate the arrival of the Halberstams' autumn guest, a tiny english duchess of indeterminate years. Madge Halberstam never failed to make a fool of herself around anyone with an English accent. Christy stared across the room and took in the sight of Tom Halberstam talking with a group of his cronies. Then she carried her drink out toward the terrace.

Every year the Halberstams had A Somebody as their fall guest. Last year it had been the rich manufacturer of Italian sports cars; the year before, a pretender to some Balkan throne. Even from the terrace she could hear the drone of voices, especially Madge's. There was something desperate about the Halberstams, the way they clamored for special guests, the parties they threw.

Now Christy set her drink down on the terrace wall and looked toward the woods in the distance. Beyond the ring of trees was a stretch of silvery water, partly obscured by branches, which Tom Halberstam stocked with trout each year. She lit a cigarette—she never inhaled—and studied the sunlight on the lake.

"You will write something nice about her, won't you?" Madge was suddenly behind her.

"Don't I always?" Christy said.

Madge laid one pink hand on Christy's wrist. "Her family is so old, it's incrediblè. The Norman Conquest, or whatever it's called."

Christy looked back in the direction of the water. She saw something move out there, a shadow. What was it, a tree shaking? The motion of branches? She dropped her cigarette underfoot, crushed it, listening to Madge make sighing noises.

"I wonder if her sense of family history is a weight," Madge said.

Christy saw it again, a shadow between the trees, a dark decal pressed upon the light. She was about to mention it to her hostess, but Madge was still going on about the duchess, her voice rising and falling in rhapsodies.

And then the duchess herself appeared, moving her head from side to side as if she were surveying peasants from the window of her carriage. Christy glanced at her watch: she'd have to leave pretty soon to get her column in on time. The weight of the deadline.

Suddenly she was impatient—she was forever colliding with the feeling that what she did was inconsequential, that her column was nothing more than fluff in a world where truly dark events took place. Wars and rapes and terrorist attacks. Her little universe was different, filled with good clothes and rich blood. She looked back in the direction of the trees one more time. Something appeared to glint out there, glass maybe. The lens of a camera. She wasn't sure of anything from this distance.

Madge said, "She must have been very beautiful as a young woman, don't you think?"

Christie looked at the duchess's face but she couldn't see any vestige of beauty there.

"I have to get going, Madge," she said.

"You promise you'll write something nice?"

"I swear—"

"And you will mention Tom's new library? He's very proud of it." Madge took Christy's hand. "It's been a pleasure, dear. As it always is."

Christie walked to the end of the terrace and down the steps. Before she turned around the side of the house she glanced back one more time toward the trees.

Nothing.

Nobody moved.

She saw only the still trees and the tantalizing suggestion of placid water beyond.

He let the binoculars fall against his chest, feeling the leather strap chafe the back of his neck. Then he moved a little further into the woods. At his back, the lake—a small oval of water surrounded by pine—made soft whispering sounds as it lapped the reeds round the shoreline.

Now he had a better view of the house. He raised the binoculars to his eyes, adjusted the lenses, trained his sight on the terrace.

He brought the woman into view.

He recognized her yellow hair and the dark dress she wore. He thought it was a little too somber for her: she shouldn't dress in charcoal grays or blacks, she should

3

wear something more celebratory, more colorful. She had turned her face in his direction a moment, then she'd looked away. Another woman was standing at her side. A conversation was taking place. He knew from the expression on her face that she wasn't altogether interested in what her companion had to say. A typical party conversation, idle chitchat. Then he dropped the binoculars and rubbed his eyes: he had made a mental list over the last few days, a catalog of the places where the woman regularly went.

Her house. Of course. And the railroad station where she picked up her husband every night of the week.

The office of the newspaper, the Chronicle.

The supermarket.

A gourmet shop, a so-called food boutique where she purchased imported items—cheeses, wines, oriental foodstuffs.

And the bar called The Dying Swan, a place where she sometimes stopped on her way home from the office.

All this had been easy to find out.

He saw that she was moving now, leaving the party, walking toward the end of the terrace. She moved with a grace he found touching, as if she were unconscious of her body, set apart from it. He watched her dress cling to her thighs—it had to be silk, something soft—and the way her hair, which was long and curled by an expensive hairdresser (he knew which one), rose and fell slightly against her shoulders. She was beautiful, desirable.

But it wasn't her beauty that intrigued him.

And it wasn't her desirability that drew him toward her.

He put his hands in his pockets. She'd disappeared around the side of the house now, but he did not rush to follow her. There wasn't much point.

4

He always knew where she was going.

He smiled to himself and he thought that if he'd wanted to kidnap her, it would have been the easiest thing in the whole world.

But he had other plans.

The sun had suddenly gone and the water was gray, depressing to him. It reminded him of something in his childhood—an elusive memory he couldn't quite track down even if he wanted to. His childhood was something he left alone, a sealed trunk whose padlock he could never allow himself to break open.

He walked the shoreline for a time, waiting for the sun to come back. But the water remained sluggishly gray, like a large sewer into which all light had sunk.

Rossiter was a small man with a head too large for his body. He was sloppy in a way Christy found endearing, his shirt buttons forever opening of their own accord, his laces coming undone as if by a force of gravity. He had been editor of the *Chronicle* for eighteen years.

Christy gazed across his desk at the mounds of orange peels, empty Dr. Pepper cans, bundles of paper in disarray. She wondered how he ever managed to find anything—but he always did: he had his own indecipherable system, beyond the understanding of all the secretaries who came and went. She watched him toss her copy aside, then peer at her over the top of his glasses.

"I can't imagine our little world without gossip," he said. "What a perfectly dull place it would be, right? We'd never get to learn anything about the number of books in Tom Halberstam's library or such shattering events as where

5

Mr. and Mrs. Globetrotter spent the summers of their discontent, would we?"

Christy understood how much her editor disliked the social world she wrote about. Still, the column—which appeared three times a week—contributed enormously to the circulation of the *Chronicle*, and Rossiter knew it.

Now he stood, looking somehow smaller than when he was seated behind his desk.

"A la-di-da duchess this time," he went on. "One day I'd like to run a check on the credentials of those parasites who come to visit our friends the Halberstams."

Rossiter walked to the window of his office, stepping over the sleeping lump that was Tarzan, the office cat.

"Lemme ask you a biggie, Christy," he said.

She waited, scratching her calf lazily. She knew what was coming, she knew it was going to be a conversation Rossiter indulged in every two or three months: for some reason, he felt a responsibility for her career, as if the onus of instilling ambition into her was his alone.

"Lemme ask you if you're happy doing what you do?"

"It's okay," she said.

"The old grapevine of rumor and gossip that runs through the blood of our fair county still enthralls you?"

"It doesn't enthrall me—"

Rossiter turned, smiling at her. "Then why don't you let me put you in another slot—"

Christy sighed. "I don't think so."

"Look at what you'd get, Christy. The chance to cover City Hall. The local politics of Bristol. All the fun and games the boys over at City Hall get up to. All the rivalries, drawn daggers, the gunshots, the marvelous infighting. How can you pass up an opportunity like that?"

6

"I don't have the time to do it, that's all. I couldn't work it into my schedule."

Rossiter made a tired gesture with his hand. "Women who work on newspapers shouldn't get married. They shouldn't set up home and try to juggle their conjugal responsibilities with their careers."

"I like my marriage," Christy said.

"You haven't been at it long enough to feel otherwise. You've also become a clock-watcher. Consider the staid years that lie in front of you. Consider the babes as yet unborn. Consider a lifetime of writing matchless prose—"

"Consider the time," she said as she looked at her watch.

"Hubby time. Let's run to the railroad station and pick up our master, shall we?"

Christy smiled at the little man. "You never stop trying, do you?"

"It's not in my nature," Rossiter said. "My trouble is, I have the heart of a bastard and the balls of a lamb. Go on. Keep writing about the degenerate social happenings that pass as big events in Bristol County. Keep hurrying to the railroad to meet the man. See if I care."

Christy looked across the newsroom a moment, watching a couple of reporters stare at the screens of the word processors Rossiter had reluctantly installed a month ago. She turned when she heard the sound of his voice.

"Know something, Christy?"

"Tell me."

"You're damn good at what you do."

She smiled again and pulled the door shut: it wasn't exactly a compliment. You're damn good at what you do, even if it *is* the most trivial thing imaginable. She went down the stairs and hurried across the parking lot to where

7

she'd left her Jaguar. As she turned on the ignition she thought of the copy she'd just handed in.

Tom Halberstam's library was "extensive."

The Duchess of Clydesdale was "engrossing" and "cosmopolitan."

These were the kinds of words her readers wanted. They wouldn't have been happy with anything else. They didn't want to look in a social column and find out about human misery unless it was disguised beneath the trappings of a charity ball.

She drove her car across Main and in the direction of Bristol Station, where Zachary's train arrived every evening at 6:06. Okay, maybe Rossiter thought what she did was frivolous in the extreme, and maybe he was right in trying to convince her to become involved in something that had more meat—but what he failed to realize was that she had her life in order, she had managed to create an equilibrium between home and marriage and work—and she liked having things under control.

It wasn't as if she were a neatness freak, the sort of woman who was forever making lists or sticking lables on the sides of spice jars: she liked order only as it applied to the important things in her world, not the trivial.

How could a man who kept his desk like the county trash dump understand the convenience of order anyhow?

She parked in the station parking lot.

In the distance she could hear the sound of Zachary's train and feel tiny reverberations under her feet.

It was a dull manuscript and Zachary was glad when the railroad station loomed up ahead because it meant he could put the thing away, stuff it into his leather briefcase and

8

forget all about it until morning. He glanced at the title page before he closed the folder. *The Search for Hilda*. It was supposed to be a thriller, something he would normally have delegated to one of the junior editors (if the goddamn thing had ever made it through the slush pile, which was doubtful), but in this case he'd felt obliged to look it over himself because it had been written, albeit pseudonymously, by one of the most famous writers on his company's list.

Zachary snapped his case shut and looked through the window of the carriage: he felt a vague ache in his stomach, a touch of mild indigestion, but it wasn't because of anything he'd eaten. It was strictly on account of Leonora's letter, which he carried in the inside pocket of his jacket.

Leonora's letters always had the same effect on him. If he was perfectly honest with himself he knew it was because she made him feel a curious kind of fear—her handwriting, dark-inked and large-lettered, struck him as a form of reprimand in itself. It was as if he'd somehow misbehaved and her letters were a sharp rap across his knuckles. He got up from his seat and saw the tiny string of lights along the platform. He was annoyed with himself for letting Leonora affect him this way. Was it a sign of some kind of weakness in him?

There was Christy waving at him. Suddenly he felt quite different: the stresses of the day—several bloodthirsty literary agents, a tense lunch with an irritable author, and Leonora's letter not least—all these things abruptly fell away from him. Christy, he thought: it's true what they say, it's true that such a simple thing as loving can change a person's life, can make it glow, cause it to be worthwhile.

She came across the platform, hugged him, smiled. Her skin was cold against the side of his face. He slipped a hand into hers, enjoying the contact between them. The station lamps glowed in her yellowy hair, lit her eyes, seemed to create a faint warm nimbus around her entire body. Nothing in his whole life, nothing in his dreams, mattered to him as much as Christy. And nothing in his experience had ever prepared him for the nature of this love.

They passed together through the gates, crossed the parking lot. He looked upward at the sky a moment. Darkening—there was a scent of winter in the air, a sharp edge, cutting.

Christy was looking at him with an affectionate smile. "Well? Do I get to hear about your day in the warrens and cubbyholes of Manhattan, Zack?"

She opened the door of her Jaguar, a flash of dull maroon in the station lights, and he slung his briefcase inside the car. "I think I've come to the understanding that I have a gentleman's agreement with the city. If I say nothing bad about it behind its back, it won't harm me, I won't get mugged or run over by an insane taxicab or thrown out of a window by a deranged writer—"

Christy slid into the driver's seat. Zachary sat down alongside her and listened a moment to the hesitant rhythm of the engine; the car became a sanctuary, a private place where he could be alone with her. You worry, he thought. You worry about those parties and functions she attends, you imagine she might meet another man somewhere along the way, a face seen over a cocktail glass, a certain look in the eyes, a movement of mouth—you let these things accumulate in your mind like so much garbage. . . . He reached out and stroked the back of her hand.

"What about your day?" he asked.

"The Halberstams. Need I say more?"

"Who is it this time?"

"A duchess."

"Where do they dig these people up?"

"Sometimes I think there's a company in Europe that hires out dignitaries for the gratification of rich Americans," Christie said, laughing.

Zachary was silent a moment. He felt a vague pain at the back of his head: it lay there, buried in the center of his skull, like a fist muffled by a glove. It was that letter again. He wished she hadn't written. It was his own fault—when he'd seen the handwriting he should never have opened the envelope. Didn't she realize that he had a life of his own to lead now? But you couldn't throw away anything of Leonora's. You never ignored Leonora.

"Maybe they like to come here to watch the fall colors," he said. "Maybe that's the attraction."

"I think it's the free food and being the center of all the attention." Christy had stopped the car at a red light and turned to look at him. "Are you okay?"

"I'm fine . . . a little hungry, maybe."

"You want to eat out? Stay home? I could fix us something—"

He was about to say that anything at all would be fine, but then he started to think about crowded restaurants and the attentions of wine stewards and the clucking of those waiters who always seemed to be lingering at her shoulder as if they were waiting for her to drop her handkerchief. "I'd like to eat at home tonight, if that's okay with you."

The light changed, the car lurched forward. He rested his head against the back of his seat and shut his eyes. Even so, he couldn't stop certain phrases from Leonora's letter entering his mind as if they were scavenger insects forever forging forward. Dark insects . . .

. . . I don't think it's a step you should have taken without consulting me, Zachary . . . I have feelings too . . .

He forced himself to stop remembering, and, leaning forward in his seat, smiling at Christy, slid one hand between the buttons of her jacket and began to massage her breasts very gently.

She looked at him: "If you're not careful—"

"I know, you'll wreck the car—"

"Right, I'll wreck the car—"

"And we'll end up in a hospital—"

"Right—"

"And then where would we be?"

"In segregated sickrooms, my love, that's where," she said.

He lowered his hand and stroked the flat of her stomach, gathering up the material of her dress between his fingers.

"Ten minutes, Zack. Ten minutes and we'll be home."

"Patience was never one of my virtues. I've always been impetuous." A statement he knew to be untrue; until Christy had come into his life every act had been weighed, every possible consequence analyzed: his had always been a dogged, unexciting approach to life.

"Five minutes," she said.

"I'm synchronizing my watch," he answered, and let his hand fall against her inner thigh, an expanse of skin so smooth and delicate he sometimes imagined that the least touch would bruise it.

12

Five minutes, he thought.

And closed his eyes again, although this time he wasn't remotely thinking about Leonora's letter.

A light in an upstairs window. A shadow seeming to melt across glass.

He watched for a while, gazing at the light, longing to see the shadow again. But it didn't come. He sat down in the dark grass and rubbed the palms of his hands together.

The house: what could you say about the place?

It was big, way too big for only two people, and it looked ponderous, ungainly, hacked out of gray stone. He thought it the kind of house a successful publisher might live in, imposing, secure, surrounded by several acres of trees, reached by a curving gravel drive. And close enough to the station to make Manhattan accessible.

Secure? Maybe.

Maybe not.

He stared at the two cars parked in the long driveway. Her wine-colored Jaguar and his little Toyota. The husband could afford something better than that. Something grand— a Daimler, a Rolls, something with style and elegance. But no, he had to be low-key. Unpretentious.

He stood up and wiped blades of grass from his pants.

And he thought how easy it would be to enter that big gray stone house, gain access through a downstairs window, climb upward to the bedroom and stand there in the dark watching the woman sleep. But that wasn't in his plans.

He tore a leaf from a tree and shredded it between his fingers as if he were nervous. But he wasn't nervous in the

13

least, he never had been, his nerve and control were things he knew he could always count on.

Qualities that had never let him down.

Christy.

He whispered her name to himself a couple of times.

Christy.

And he turned away from the house, imagining for a moment the sight of Christy lying under her husband's body, imagining her nakedness pressed against his, her hair flattened against a pillow. Did she make sounds? Little noises? Did she whimper and whine into her husband's ear as she locked her ankles against the flat of his back?

He realized he didn't know the answers to these questions.

But it didn't matter.

Because he'd have the answers anytime he liked.

And that time would be soon.

2

Coldwind disliked his visits to the Huntington home. As soon as he parked his car outside the elaborate entrance to the place and grimaced at the statues flanking the door, he felt the spring going out of his step and a certain dryness at the back of his throat. The statues, for one thing—he'd try to pass them quickly, hurrying up the steps to the door, but today he paused long enough to take them in.

They had been hewn out of marble by a sculptor who must have had an affinity with the nether regions of nightmare: twisted faces, contorted limbs, arthritic poses, every figure suggesting pain of an intensely private nature. Coldwind was glad that his business at the Huntington home never took place after dark. A lawyer by profession and an unimaginative man by inclination, the prospect of stumbling across these monstrosities at night nevertheless appalled him. And then there was the house itself; its gloomy corners and dim passageways unnerved him more than he was prepared to admit.

He rang the brass doorbell and waited, briefcase clutched to his side: the knowledge that it contained various legal papers consoled him—at least there was nothing ambiguously fearful about such documents. When Skyler, the butler, opened the door Coldwind hesitated a moment before going in. Maybe it was simply a case of nerves, but there was something about Skyler that he found disconcerting too—as if, after years of service to the Huntingtons, elements of this gloomy old house had rubbed off on the old man. The papery skin, the dark circles beneath the eyes, the colorless lips: one could imagine that Skyler slept in an icebox.

Coldwind moved along the hallway, sensing the butler at his back. I do not like coming here, he told himself. I most certainly do not like it. He stopped outside the closed double doors of the library and let Skyler push them open, and then he was inside the big room filled with musty books and antique wall maps. Skyler withdrew and Coldwind sat down, briefcase in his lap. Although the room was hot he didn't take off his coat, didn't attempt to loosen the knot of his tie. He waited, as he usually did, for the appearance of Mrs. Huntington.

It isn't the house that's getting to me, he thought.

It's the business that brings me here.

He fidgeted with the clasp of his briefcase and then he heard the sound of the doors opening, the swish of Mrs. Huntington's long skirt against the wall. He turned. She was, as ever, beautiful. It was an odd kind of beauty, though—Coldwind always felt as if he were seeing the woman through cheesecloth, her features slightly blurred, a face lit by a considerate cameraman. Had he not known that she was forty-three, it would have been impossible to guess her age.

She drifted across the room, the navy-blue dress touching the rug, and smiled at him in her pale way.

He began to rise; with a gesture of her hand she implied that it wasn't necessary to stand on her behalf. She smiled again and moved behind the desk, one hand spinning a globe of the world as she passed it.

"You have the papers," she said.

Coldwind opened his briefcase. He wanted to speak but his throat was still very dry. As he handed her the papers he was filled with a sudden longing to be back in his office, surrounded by the violence of ringing telephones, the rush of junior partners, the swirl of secretaries—life, he thought, he wanted to touch life and be surrounded by it. Anything but this.

Mrs. Huntington skipped through the papers. Coldwind knew she was reading them even though she gave an impression of carelessness. And then he wondered why, after all the years he had served the Huntingtons, he'd never called the woman by her first name. It had never seemed appropriate; Mrs. Huntington lived on another plane to which he was denied access—he had no other explanation for it.

"I need your signature at the bottom of each page," he said finally.

"Of course."

He watched the movement of a pen in her hand. She held it as if she weren't really touching it. He massaged the sides of his head a moment: he had to bring the matter up sooner or later. There would never be a truly good time for it, so, in one of the more uninhibited actions of his life, he cleared his throat and spoke up.

17

"Mrs. Huntington, I really don't see the point in prolonging a situation—"

Those eyes, he thought.

It was the way she turned them on him: the look, which pierced him like a lance, made him feel as though he was coming undone. He felt his composure fade and knew there were spots of perspiration on his brow.

What had ever prompted him to speak up? He was no more Mrs. Huntington's equal than Skyler, the butler— probably even less. He cleared his throat and stared at her and saw that she was smiling at him now. It struck him that for years he had been more than a little in love with this woman—the kind of love that only flourishes when its sentiments go unsaid. An adolescent thing, stuffed with hopeless longings. It wasn't anything he paused to consider frequently. Now the palms of his hands were damp.

"Certan arrangements are necessary in a situation like this, Mr. Coldwind," she said, and one hand went up toward her hair. He longed to grasp that hand and press his lips against it. "Discretion is something missing from our everyday lives, don't you think? And I have always considered you the very soul of discretion, Mr. Coldwind."

She stood, and suddenly she seemed very large to the lawyer, filling this room, her smile expanding until it lit every dark corner of the place. There was a vague scent of her perfume, understated but touching him as surely as a bird's wing.

"I have certain responsibilities," she said.

"As we all have—"

"You know what mine are, Mr. Coldwind. Don't you?"

Something in the way she'd bitten off the question made him feel a vague pricking of fear. He moved toward the door, lingering there even if he didn't want to. Secrets, he thought, lawyers are entrusted with secrets, and sometimes they become too heavy, they become enormous piles of unwashed laundry you want desperately to get rid of, only you know you can't do it, you're pledged to carry them for a very long time.

She was coming across the floor toward him. She laid one hand on the back of his wrist. Her skin was warm: he'd imagined ice. He trembled very slightly.

"You're forgetting the papers," she said.

"The papers, of course," and he took them from her, thrusting them inside his briefcase like burning coals. "I'd forget my head sometimes . . ."

"If it wasn't attached to your neck," she offered.

"Indeed."

She accompanied him along the hallway to the front door. He felt the need once again to say something, but he didn't. Her nearness was suffocating him and he was delighted when she moved in front of him and held the door open— trees, sky, the sound of distant traffic, these things filled him with joy all at once.

At the bottom of the steps he turned and looked up at the sight of her standing in the doorway. Standing in front of the monstrous statues.

The way she looked—

Even though her eyes were fixed on him, she seemed not to see him at all.

There were small bowls of goat's cheese, olives, shredded salads, moussaka. Christy sipped on her ouzo and listened to the music of the Greek band which sat in a dark alcove at the back of the room. The owner, a certain Mr.

19

Gastopolous, was threading his way through the crowd toward her, a cigar in one hand, a glass in the other. "Kreesty, Kreesty," he was saying. "How you think? You think my restaurant is going to be a winner in our city?"

Christy put her glass down on the table and felt the big man's hand rub her shoulder. The restaurant, called the Lord Byron, was the first Greek place in Bristol. It was done in white stucco and there were Greek letters painted in a childlike hand along the walls.

"How you think, Kreesty?"

"It's going to be an outrageous success, Mr. Gastopolous," she said. "I'm sure of it."

"You will mention my enterprise in your newspaper?"

Christy nodded; the Greek's hand was still pumping her shoulder. She pushed her hair away from her face and reached for her glass.

"You will say the nicest things? My chef has come all the way from Athens. A man of temperament. He likes praise. You know how that is." The Greek smiled. He had dark, rather soulful eyes and his smile was touched a little with sadness. Christy glanced a moment at the band and shifted herself out from under Gastopolous's hand.

"Circulate, Kreesty," the Greek was saying. "Feel free to wander in the kitchen. Speak with my chef. Go anywhere you like—" And then Gastopolous was gone, to work the rest of the room, his voice carrying over the music. Christy finished her drink and looked at the other guests, who stood around nibbling olives or forking chunks of moussaka into their mouths. There were a couple of dignitaries from City Hall, a smattering of journalists—including the restaurant critic of the *Bristol Eye*, the city's alternative newspaper— several restaurateurs, a dozen or so people from what might

loosely be called the city's social set. At one time or another,
Christy had run into everybody in the room.

Except one.

He was standing alone near the doorway, a man of about
thirty, well-dressed in a lightweight blue suit, his navy-blue
shirt open at the neck. He had his hands in the pockets of his
pants, and apart from the few times he looked in Christy's
direction, seemed quite uninterested in the proceedings
around him. She watched him a moment and found herself
thinking: He's gorgeous—a word that she rarely used, even
in the privacy of her thoughts. He had long fair hair swept
back across his head. There was something a little sullen
about his mouth, something moody, as if he wished himself
elsewhere and was here only under sufferance. Christy filled
her glass with ouzo and wandered toward the musicians,
who suddenly grew animated, showing off for her. She
smiled at their silliness; then she was conscious of the
young man approaching her, crossing the room and standing
some feet away from her. Sipping her drink, she turned to
glance at him over the rim of her glass.

He moved past her, plucked an olive from a bowl, placed
it on his tongue. Then he smiled at her. She was flustered all
at once, without knowing why. The music, the ouzo, the
smile—a conspiracy of things. Then he was standing
alongside her, so close she could smell his cologne.

"We've never met," he said. "My name's Richie."

She realized she was tapping her wedding ring against the
side of her glass. "Christy McNair," she said, very
conscious of the noise of gold upon glass, a tiny drumbeat.
She put her drink down on the table.

"What brings you here?" he asked.

"My newspaper column," she answered.

21

"You're a scribbler?"

"A scribbler," she said. "I've never been called that before."

"What do you write?" he asked, his eyes never moving from her face.

"A social column. The *Chronicle*."

"The *Bristol Chronic*," he said.

She laughed; even among its staffers, the *Chronicle* was always known by its derogatory nickname. "What do you do, Richie?" she asked.

"I'm a hobbyist."

"Which sounds cryptic."

"Does it? It wasn't meant to. I like to watch people."

"Does somebody pay you to do that?"

"I do it for free."

She looked at him quickly, then turned her face to the side. I like to watch people—what kind of response was that anyhow? Maybe he belonged to the idle rich, to old Bristol money; he looked like a bored aristocrat. But then why wasn't he fraternizing with the rest of his crowd? Why wasn't he standing around with that bunch? It was flattering that he was giving her his attention. Most women would have been thrilled by so handsome a man conversing with them, but she'd never been drawn by physical beauty in the past, preferring relationships with people she found interesting because of their experiences or their intelligence. Besides, she thought, you're a married woman and happily so, and you don't run around getting off on the notion of good-looking young men paying attention to you.

She turned her thoughts deliberately to Zachary, and tried to imagine him in his office in Manhattan, surrounded by manuscripts, contracts, galleys, his telephone ringing. For a second she could envisage his serious face and intense expression, remembering now that it was exactly that quality of intensity that had attracted her to him in the first place. He had given her the impression of hidden depths, secret places in his mind, little rooms to which she wanted to gain access. And a strange, quiet strength as well, something she felt she could tap if she ever needed to. She had always imagined spending her life getting to know him. Getting to understand him in gradual, delightful ways. She even found his small insecurities charming for the most part: they made her feel as if she were the single most important thing in his life.

"What does watching people entail?" she asked.

"Looking. Getting a sense of things. Understanding their qualities."

"It sounds too mysterious for me."

He smiled at her: she felt as if he suddenly approved of her. Why did something so simple as a smile have the effect at times of an electric light going on in a black room?

"I didn't mean to sound enigmatic," he said. "I'm between things at the moment. I'm just looking around, trying to decide what to do."

Between things, she thought. This was the way an actor might talk: I'm between plays at the moment. Certainly he was good-looking enough to be an actor, and he had an easy charm of the kind she'd noticed in other actors she'd met, as if he were confident and comfortable with himself.

"You're going to write about this place?" he asked.

"Yes."

"You find yourself at this kind of function often?"

"A lot of the time," she said.

He plucked another olive from the table and stuck it

inside his mouth, chewing on it with a thoughtful look. "Doesn't it get tedious?"

"Sometimes." She shrugged.

"I imagine in a place like Bristol you keep running into the same people, don't you? The same little social set. They're quite an inbred bunch."

"You seem to know a lot about this city. Do you live around here?"

"I travel. But I come back to Bristol every now and then," and he was smiling as if he found the idea of Bristol an amusing one. Maybe he's used to more cosmopolitan places, she thought, and for a moment she could imagine him strolling idly across the terrace of some expensive resort in Mexico, a white jacket slung across his shoulders, white shoes and white pants, everything blazing in the terrible sunlight. She could see women turning their heads, studying him from behind the safety of black glasses.

Mr. Gastopolous was coming back across the room.

"Well, Kreesty? What do you think?"

"It's really very pleasant," she said.

"We try. A lot of effort. A lot of cash investment."

Christy nodded. She watched Richie drift away, go toward the door, watched the door swing open as he moved out to the street—and for one weird moment she wanted to call him back. Gastopolous was massaging her shoulder again, his hand as heavy as a bear's paw. Like a trap, she thought.

The door, in a glint of light, swung shut.

"The people of Bristol will like Greek food," Gastopolous said. "They will like it very much."

"I'm sure—" She looked at the Greek a moment. "Do you know anything about that young man who was here?"

"Only one thing," he said. "He was not invited."

24

* * *

Zachary listened to the wind sough through the trees, to how it made the house creak as if it were not built of solid masonry but something flimsy on stilts at the edge of a beach. He put down his manuscript and walked over to the French windows that looked out across the lawn. A gray day, clouds scudding across the skyline. Trees shivering in the wind. A storm, he thought. An autumn storm was blowing up. He saw Christy's Jaguar come slowly along the driveway and then, because he didn't want her to think he'd been watching for her return, he went back to his chair and picked up the manuscript.

It was a historical work about the Crusades. He was happier with history than he was with fiction: he could bury himself more easily in reconstructions of the past than in reconstructions of reality. He heard her car door slam shut, pictured her walking up the steps, getting the front door open, stepping inside. And then something slightly dark crossed his mind, something that had the texture of a rusty old razor blade. She's been to another of her social gatherings, another opportunity to meet new people, fresh faces. You have to get around this stumbling block, you have to stop putting obstacles in front of your heart, he said to himself. You have to keep reminding yourself that she is your wife. Maturity: that was the name of the quality to which he aspired.

Zachary McNair, thirty-six years of age, and suffused with maturity. He put down his pen and looked at her as she entered the room. And he suddenly remembered how he had first met Christy—it had been at one of those functions, an autograph party for one of his authors.

One of those functions, he thought.

He smiled at her. She was slightly drunk—no, drunk was too harsh a word: tipsy, that was what he wanted. Her face was a little flushed and her eyes glazed.

"Remind me not to drink ouzo," she said. "It doesn't agree with me."

"Beware of Greeks," he said.

She nodded: "What are you reading?"

"A history of bloodiness," he said. "Did you eat?"

"A little." She swung one leg back and forth; she was wearing a velvet dress and high-heeled boots.

The wind was rising outside, the trees rattling harder. Zachary closed the windows as Christy slumped into the armchair. He looked around the room—it was one of the few places where he felt truly secure, safe from the external world. This big comfortable room with the solid furniture and a fire burning and the hunting prints on the walls was sanctuary. He stood behind Christy and massaged her shoulders.

"How was the restaurant?"

"Crowded—"

"See anybody you know?"

"I always run into the same people," she answered. "Same people, same conversations."

The bored tone in her voice cheered him a little. "I get the feeling you'll give it up one day—"

"I might."

He ran his hands inside her shirt, touching her breasts. She raised her body upward in the chair, arching her spine, a gesture he found vaguely feline. He moved his hands further down, working them inside the belt of her pants, stroking the soft smooth surface of her stomach. The growing sense of excitement he felt was painful: he moved

26

around the front of the chair and tugged at the buckle of her belt and watched the way she had half closed her eyes as if she were stepping into a world too private for him to enter. Why, in the act of love, did it always seem to him that he was losing her? Her retreats, her hidden places: even as his excitement grew he sensed an undercurrent of his own despair. And sometimes he imagined that he didn't exist as Zachary at all, that the hands which touched her might have belonged to almost anyone, a stranger.

He drew her down on the rug, pulled at her zipper, drew her pants from her thighs. She was staring at him—she isn't seeing me, he thought, she's gone away from me, spinning off into a world of her own making. He made love to her quickly, and when he had finished he held her against him as if there were something important that he'd quite forgotten. Did it always have to be like this? Did loving always have to be bound up with an unutterable fear?

She kissed his forehead in a gentle way.

"I love you," he said.

"I know you do—"

He raised his face slightly and looked at her. He was filled with a sense of future loss, a potential loneliness he found insufferable. Love was a kind of madness, a bewildering imprisonment of consciousness.

She rolled over on her side, away from him, rummaging in her purse for a cigarette, which she lit without taking her eyes from his face.

"What is it?" she asked. "What's wrong?"

He didn't answer her at once. He rose, gazing into the fire, listening to the wind, the savage creak of the house, assailed all over again by a premonition of loss. You think the wrong way, he told himself. You see the world in terms

27

of threats, menaces, you feel a sharpening of knives out there when all you should ever consider is bright love.

He said, "Nothing's wrong . . ."

He saw uncertainty in her eyes. She couldn't be lied to, she couldn't be cheated: she saw too far inside him for that.

"Sometimes I think I'm going to lose you," he said. It was as if he had released a bird, a thing held in captivity for too long a time. She reached forward and put her hands on his shoulders and smiled.

"You've got to stop being afraid," she said.

"I try—"

"Try harder, Zachary. There's nothing to be scared of. Don't you know that?"

He closed his eyes and buried his face against her breasts.

555-3030.

He looked at the telephone number scribbled on the pad, then got up from the bed and walked to the window. He could see the hotel sign impressed upon the darkness like a neon embroidery. THE BRISTOL CONCORDE.

Five-five-five-three-oh-three-oh.

The glare of the room made his head ache. Then he was surprised by the sound of knocking on his door. He opened it cautiously; it was the maid he'd turned away earlier when she'd come to make up his bed and tidy the room—a girl of about seventeen, her thin body swamped by the cavernous maroon smocks of the hotel domestics.

She came inside, glancing at him shyly. "Can I change the sheets now?" she asked.

He nodded. He sat in the armchair by the window, drumming his fingers on the surface of the coffee table. It was raining now: he could hear it fall against the ledge. He

28

watched the girl strip the sheets from the bed, absently admiring the movement of her hips under the smock. There was a taste in his mouth—stale ouzo. In a moment he'd go into the bathroom and brush his teeth. But right now he just wanted to watch the girl. He understood he could he get out of the armchair and cross the room and press her down on the bed and she'd yield without complaint—he'd never had problems with women and he didn't anticipate any in the future.

555-3030.

He studied his fingernails. He had always been meticulous about his appearance.

The girl had completed her task and was looking at him. For a moment he was taken by her youthfulness, a certain innocence in her eyes.

"Will there be anything else?" she said.

He had a variety of answers to the question. He stood up and approached her. "What's your name?"

"Samantha," she said, a whisper.

"There's nothing else, Samantha."

She appeared a little disappointed, turning toward the door slowly.

He watched her shuffle out. Then the door was shut and he was alone again. He sat on the edge of the bed, staring at the writing on the pad. Then he picked up the phone and punched the number out. He waited. It was Christy who answered.

"Hullo? Hullo?"

He didn't speak. He simply put the receiver down and lay back across the bed, his hands folded behind his head, thinking about the way she had looked in the Greek restaurant, thinking about his next move. Which would be soon now.

29

He smiled to himself and he listened to the rain sweep across the window, remembering other rains and other rooms, weathers and locations chained to the past.

"Who was it?" Zachary asked. He was lying on the bed, the pages of his manuscript spread untidily across the blanket. Christy stood near the dressing table, conscious of her own reflection in the mirror.

"There wasn't anybody," she said.

"Nobody?"

She sat on the edge of the bed and laid a hand across his arm.

"They just hung up—"

Zachary raised his face from the manuscript. "Strange," he said.

"It happens," she said. She lifted his hand to her mouth and kissed it, then looked at him over the small pale ridges of his knuckles. Dear God, he tried so hard to hide his insecurities but he wasn't very good at it. He could be as transparent as glass, a very fine glass you had to take care not to shatter. She wondered why he chose to be this way at times—thirteen months of marriage hadn't altogether weakened the doubts and anxieties that ran like spidery cracks along the surface of their life together. She lay down alongside him, running a hand through his hair. He had very pale skin, almost translucent; she could see blue veins beneath the surface.

"It was a wrong number," she said.

"I guess . . ."

He shrugged and turned his face toward the manuscript; it was one of those tomes with footnotes, the kind he always seemed inordinately fond of—dense paragraphs and arcane references. She tried to see inside his mind a moment. Why, when he could be so loving, did he allow his occasional suspicions to interrupt the course of their marriage? He knows that I love him, she thought, he has to know that much by this time.

She placed her hand beneath his robe and rubbed his hip, making small circles with her hand. "Look, the telephone rings. The person on the other end doesn't answer. It's a pretty common occurrence. There's nothing sinister about it."

"Did I say I thought there was anything sinister about it?"

She shook her head, running her fingers along his leg, from the crook of the knee to the upper thigh. "Make love to me, Zack—"

She saw him close his eyes. Maybe this was the only way to make him feel good, to ease whatever ridiculous concerns he might have.

"Zack . . ."

She put her hand between his legs. She watched pages of the manuscript flutter to the floor as he rolled toward her.

He slipped the robe from her shoulders and, moaning softly, placed his mouth between her breasts. She turned over on her back and then his weight was pressed against her and she spread her legs, feeling him settle inside her, hearing him whisper in her ear, nonwords, love sounds, nothing that would make any sense to anyone but her. She folded her arms around him: it was good, it was good and sweet, this intimacy, this privacy.

When the telephone rang again, neither of them heard it.

She woke, thirsty from the ouzo, and went downstairs, careful not to rouse Zachary. There was a tiny throbbing pain at the sides of her head and she was sleepy. Inside the kitchen she filled a glass with water, drank quickly, then carried her glass out into the study. Outside, the night was utterly still, the moon a faint crescent assailed by motionless clouds. She looked across the lawn to the distant trees.

Something was moving out there.

A dog, perhaps. Or maybe some foraging animal from the woods beyond Bristol, something that had strayed from its usual habitat. She watched for a while, her eyes following the shadowy figure as it made its way beneath dark branches.

Then it was gone.

She hauled the drapes across the windows and moved out of the study to the stairs. Zachary was standing at the top, lit only by the light from the bedroom at his back.

"Something wrong?" he asked.

"I was thirsty."

She stopped again halfway up, adding: "Remind me not to drink ouzo in the future."

Inside the bedroom she gazed up at the dark ceiling. An animal of some kind, she thought. Something that had come to feed in the mysterious reaches of night.

3

"We're going to have to reschedule," Tully said. He picked up a folder from Zachary's desk and flipped through it. "If Manley can't deliver before Jan One, we can't publish by summer."

Zachary, barely listening, glanced at his watch. It was almost noon and he was anxious to be gone from his office. He looked at Tully, taking in the long thin body, the thin white hands, the nose that always seemed to collect a tiny drop of moisture at its tip. Tully was senior editor at Dackson, McNair, a company that Zachary had bought five years ago from its founder, Laird Dackson, an inebriated bibliophile whose publishing operation was languishing because Dackson, even in moments of sobriety, was unable to acquire new books. Zachary had managed to turn the company around—a combination of dogged hard work, a willingness to court literary agents, and a twist of good fortune in some of his publishing choices. He tipped his chair back now and looked around his office, trying to tune Tully out; if there was one thing about the business that bored Zachary it was the matter of scheduling—Tully, on the other hand, dreamed of schedules in his sleep.

Zachary stood up, his hands in his pockets, and went to the window—there was a view of Forty-second Street, cabs passing, pedestrians dodging rain puddles. But he wasn't really seeing any of these things. Instead, he was imagining how, behind this fabric of normality, there was another world—a place of spectral appearances, faint apparitions, the swirling of shapeless suspicions.

"There's also the matter of the new Bernhardt," Tully was saying.

"You can never expect Dick Bernhardt to produce anything on time," Zachary said.

Tully sniffed, wiped the tip of his nose with a bony finger. "I don't see why we put delivery dates in our contracts if people like Dick Bernhardt can't stick with them." Zachary looked at his watch again. Twelve-oh-five. As he took his raincoat from the peg on the wall, the intercom on his desk buzzed. He heard Sally's nasal tones. "Zack, there's somebody called Leonora for you on line three."

Leonora. "I'm out," Zachary said.

"She's pissed at something, I can tell you that—"

"I'll get back to her."

Zachary buttoned his coat and looked at Tully. "I've got an appointment. We can pick this up this afternoon."

With a tidy gesture Tully tucked his folder beneath his arm and walked to the door. "What time?" he asked.

"Three-thirty." Zachary picked up his umbrella and raced to the elevators. He dreaded the confinement of the small cages, the relentless sound of Muzak that assailed his ears. He rode all the way to the ground floor with his eyes shut. Then he was out in the street, walking in the direction of Fifth Avenue. He turned north toward Central Park, his pace even; he barely noticed the soft rain and he didn't open his umbrella. Only when he saw the entrance to the park did he slow his movements—what did he feel? he wondered. A sense of shame? He paused and looked through the trees, listening to the whispering noise of rain against leaves. Leonora, he thought: the letter, now a telephone call. He had an image suddenly of Leonora's face, a picture he pushed aside dismissively. He didn't need to think about Leonora now, even if he knew she wasn't going to go away easily. She never did.

He moved along a pathway, pausing again when he saw that Rucker was already waiting for him on the bench. He wanted to turn around and step away, step back from this encounter, pretend he had never set in motion such a train of events. But it was too late because Rucker, a fat man in a large raincoat, had already seen him and was waving a rolled-up newspaper. Slowly Zachary approached the bench and sat down.

Rucker, who had a puffy face with small eyes buried in tiny mounds of flesh, struck the side of the bench with the newspaper, as if he were troubled by imaginary flies. Zachary poked at pebbles with the tip of his umbrella: it was more than embarrassing, he thought, it was perfectly hideous. He wished he were back in his office going through the boring schedules with Tully. Rucker spoke in a voice made harsh and throaty by cigarettes. It was a late-night voice, the kind that you would expect to hear at the other end of an obscene phone call. Zachary began to draw a circle with his umbrella in the soft soil. A phone call, he remembered: Christy had picked up the receiver and said something he hadn't been able to catch, something quick

35

and breathless. Then she'd hung up, after which it seemed to him that she'd gone to some lengths to dismiss the matter. He sighed: it's nothing, I am making substances out of nothing. And he wondered, as he often did, what kind of man he was that he'd be driven into the clutches of somebody like Rucker. What kind of man was so upset by a wrong number on a telephone, for heaven's sake?

You could fight these feelings. You don't need to give in to them the way you do. You don't need to feel the past rise up like some wild beast and destroy you like this.

Rucker had large red hands he turned over; deep lines crossed his palms like gullies on a contour map. "I don't know what it is you expect, Mr. McNair. What you expect me to turn up—"

Zachary said nothing for a time; he felt that if he spoke he would somehow incriminate himself.

"What do you usually look for in such situations?" he finally asked.

"The word would be indiscretions," Rucker said. "Do you have good reason to suspect such things?"

"I believe that's your province," Zachary said.

"Ah, well." Rucker was examining his hands: patches of dry skin clung to the base of his thumbs. "Sometimes it helps in advance if we know—even vaguely—what we're supposed to be looking for."

"I can't really say anything else, Mr. Rucker."

"I understand."

Zachary stood up. He'd been here too long already; if he were to linger even a moment longer he would be tainted further.

"I have your number, Mr. McNair."

"The office only, of course."

36

"Of course," Rucker said.

Rucker stood up. He was leaning toward Zachary, creating a certain intimacy that Zachary didn't feel happy about: a bond of suspicion, woven here in the rain.

"You understand, Mr. McNair, that my company takes considerable pride in being discreet—"

"Yes," Zachary said.

"As confidential as any confessional," Rucker added.

Is he trying to make me feel uneasy? Guilty? Zachary stepped away and, as much to hide his face from Rucker as to protect himself from rain, opened out his umbrella.

"What we say between us goes no further, Mr. McNair."

Zachary was already walking away from the man, moving back toward Fifth Avenue. He paused at a red light, unconscious of people milling around him. Something had been broken here, something twisted, snapped: what in the name of God have I gone and done?

My world and Rucker's, he thought: what have I done to make them collide like this?

Since it was a day without professional obligations, no openings to report, no gossip to collect and collate, Christy rose late. She liked those mornings that stretched out in front of her with the promise of freedom, when she wasn't tied to deadlines and demands. She dressed casually in old jeans and a sweatshirt and drove down through the town of Bristol and out beyond the factory complexes toward the open countryside. There was a watery sun in the sky, and the green fields had darkened with the coming of fall, but it was a time of year she enjoyed just the same: she rolled her windows down and let the wind blow through her hair. When she came to a country inn called The Falcon she parked the Jaguar and went inside, thinking she might eat a light lunch and have one drink. She sat in the small bar, which was beamed with old wood and hung with brasses, and ordered a Scotch and water as she studied the menu.

Zack had brought her to this place a couple of times, though not recently. Back before their marriage he'd been fond of going out with her, taking her places, showing her off, but somewhere along the way, as if a discordant note had entered into an otherwise pleasant piece of music, he had stopped wanting to go out. She closed the menu and set it aside: she didn't want to spend her free day thinking about Zack's ridiculous insecurities, because what she encountered when she did was an odd sense of suffocation. His anxieties—or whatever she wanted to call them—had erected fences around their marriage. For one thing, where had all her friends gone? Why didn't they call her anymore? Why did she feel that any arrangement with her friends, any casual social gathering, was something threatening to Zachary?

She sipped her drink, lit a cigarette, let it burn in the ashtray. There was a lunchtime crowd here, a bunch of Bristol businessmen who had driven out into the country-side to escape the city at noon. They sat around a large table, laughing at something; every so often one of them would turn to look at her, as if her presence here implied something about her availability.

"Alone?"

Christy looked up, expecting to see one of the busi-nessmen standing over her table.

But it was Richie.

He sat down and smiled, clasping his hands together and leaning forward to gaze at her. "You don't mind, do you?"

"It's a small world," she said.

"That's Bristol for you. You just keep running into the same people all the time."

She considered this a moment and found herself wondering about the nature of coincidence. Yesterday he had turned up at a Greek restaurant to which he hadn't been invited; today he had abruptly materialized out of nowhere, again without an invitation. It crossed her mind that he might have followed her out here, but there was something so absurd in this idea that she had to dismiss it. Coincidences happened, after all. And Bristol, as he had pointed out, was a small world. She ran a finger around the rim of her glass.

"Can I ask you a question?" she said.

"Please do."

"What is it that you do exactly, Richie?"

"Didn't I tell you that yesterday?"

"You were mysterious yesterday."

That smile on his face, that dazzle of a smile; you could go blind looking at it.

"I didn't mean to be." He did not stop looking at her. "The truth is, I've done lots of things in my life. I've had any number of jobs. Perhaps I don't know what it is I want to do, really. A few years ago I thought I had all the time in the world to make up my mind, but time has this bad habit of passing pretty damn quickly. Which is when you start to panic and wonder about your function in life."

"This is a roundabout way of saying you're unemployed?"

He nodded. "Unemployed but not poor, you understand."

Not poor, she thought. What did that mean? An income

39

from a wealthy family background? She thought it would be impolite to ask, to pry any further. Some old Bristol families were rather furtive about their holdings and investments, keeping secrets close to their hearts with a New England tight-lipped reticence.

"Do you roam around the countryside often?" he asked.

"This is one of my days off."

He tilted his chair back against the wall and scrutinized her. He had one of those handsome faces that always appear irritatingly unmarred, the kind of face you just knew had sailed through adolescence without blemish. She imagined him strutting around a campus somewhere with a girl on each arm. Or driving a convertible that always seemed to run out of gas on lonely roads.

"Where's your husband?" he asked.

"How do you know I'm married?"

"Yesterday you were wearing a wedding ring."

And hammering it against the side of a glass as if it were a warning, she thought.

"He's working," she said.

"What does he do?"

"He's a publisher."

Richie nodded. "Your drink's empty. Want another?"

Before she could refuse, he was signaling to the waiter and a second Scotch was brought to the table. She sipped it and realized that she hadn't really wanted this second drink—the first was beginning to work inside her—but he hadn't given her the opportunity to turn it down, acting as if he wasn't accustomed to getting refusals from women. Which was probably the case, she thought. And quite suddenly, out of nowhere, she felt a vague sense of danger, as if she were skirting the edge of some flirtation with this man. As if she were turning over in her mind a fantasy that would always remain an idle one. Call it old-fashioned, but she had certain ideas about marital fidelity, namely that it was something to be treasured. Even so, as she looked at him now, she understood that if she hadn't been married she might have been intrigued by him; and then she thought of the difficulty in having a relationship with somebody this attractive—the waters would always be treacherous, always filled with sharks. Whole shimmering schools of other women basking, just waiting for a chance to bite.

Then she felt mildly guilty about this kind of speculation. It was perfectly harmless, of course, but just the same she felt she was in some odd way betraying Zachary. What if he walked into this bar right now? What would he think? What wild conclusions would he leap to? All his fears would be set on fire in one great incendiary pile.

"I have to get going," she said. She stood up and Richie rose with her.

"I'll walk outside with you," he said. No pressure, no expression of disappointment, no tiny exhortations for her to stay a little longer. She was glad of that.

She walked across the parking lot, Richie moving quietly at her side. When she reached the Jaguar she turned to him. She had the feeling he was struggling to say something, trying to drag words up from a deep place inside himself. His face appeared tense now, little lines stretched across his forehead. He's going to ask to see me again, she thought. He's going to ask me to go out with him. To meet him someplace, a quiet afternoon together.

Don't.

Don't ask me anything like that, Richie.

Let's leave it just as it is.

41

He smiled, relaxed again, as if the moment of tension had evaporated inside him.

"Well, maybe we'll run into one another again, Christy."

"Maybe so." She opened the door of her car, hesitated a moment.

Then she got inside the Jaguar and started the engine, waving at Richie as she slipped out of the parking lot.

Halfway back to Bristol, she realized there was a small sports car, an MG, some distance behind her on the narrow highway. And it occurred to her that it might be Richie's car, that he might be following her back toward the city.

On the outskirts of town she lost sight of it.

She thought: You don't even know the kind of car he drives.

And you don't know that he was following you anywhere.

But the idea stayed with her all the way home.

He lay on the bed, his hands tucked behind his head, face turned toward the window. There was late-afternoon sunlight pressed like a yellowy film across the glass. Christy, he thought. What he remembered was the way he had so unexpectedly felt desire for her—right there in that parking lot, a sudden bolt of desire. It was too soon. He stared into the palm of one hand, then began to rub his jaw. And he realized he felt slightly sorry for her: she wasn't aware of the events around her, she didn't know anything about her immediate future, she didn't understand what was going on.

Poor lovely Christy.

And poor old Zachary.

Don't start feeling sorry for the woman, because that kind of thing interferes with your ultimate goal.

He sat upright. Just the same, it isn't going to be the easiest thing in the world, not if I find myself really liking her.

But I don't.

I don't like her.

She doesn't fit. Doesn't belong. She hasn't any rights.

Why did that make him feel a certain passing sadness?

He turned when he heard the sound of a knock on the door.

It was the maid, Samantha.

"Is this a good time?" she asked.

He nodded, wondering if he might imagine that this young girl was Christy. She set fresh white sheets down alongside the bed, then she stripped the old ones in a practiced manner. He watched the way her tapered fingers smoothed the sheets, the slight swing of her smock against her buttocks and hips. Why not? he thought. Why not?

He moved across the room and, standing immediately behind her, placed his hands upon her hips. She didn't say anything: she stopped what she was doing and stood very still. He thought he could hear her heartbeat, quick as a rabbit's. He touched the back of her neck lightly with his lips and felt her shiver. The secret moment, the moment just before everything was revealed, before it was down to flesh and bone. It was always his best time. He slid his hands up under her smock and played with the edge of her panties and watched as she tilted her face back, her eyes shut, mouth halfway open. Her hands, moving behind her own back, began to stroke him and he felt aroused now, suddenly so, his blood coursing through him with an edge of fire. He turned her around to face him and saw her go down on her knees, listened to the labored sound of her breathing, felt

43

*her fingers quickly undo his pants and then he was inside
her mouth, moving against her tongue and teeth and gums.*

*He moved her away, lowered her onto the bed, unbut-
toned her smock, pushed his hands between her legs. He
thought: Christy, Christy, Christy—and then her fingernails
were digging into his back, scratching his skin, and she was
moaning beneath him as she came.*

She isn't some hotel maid. She isn't a stranger called
Samantha. She's Christy. She's Christy. *And he felt a sense
of triumph all at once, as if he'd conquered something
impossible.*

*But then the image dissolved and he was left feeling
empty and bleak and a little disgusted at what had taken
place. For a moment he wanted to hurt this young girl, he
wanted to bring her pain.*

*She lay very quiet for a time, a small smile on her face.
When she sat up he ran a fingertip down her spine.*

"You surprised me," she said in a whisper.

*He didn't speak: the silences of the aftermaths were
always labyrinths he liked to explore. Deep passageways of
quiet and solitude.*

*She was reaching for her smock, giggling suddenly like a
schoolgirl who has astonished herself by her boldness, by
her own mischief.*

*He watched her dress. She bent once and lightly kissed
the head of his cock.*

"Do you want me to come back later?" she asked.

*He didn't answer: he saw the makings of complexity here
and that was something he needed to avoid. It didn't matter:
he'd just check out of here and go to another hotel.*

"Do you?" she asked.

"I have to go out for a time."

She didn't seem remotely disappointed. She just said, "You're good," and then she was gone.

In a day or so he'd forget the girl Samantha, forget that the encounter had ever taken place, just as he'd forgotten so many others like it—scenes that took on the qualities of old dreams.

Daniel Huntington, a retired Wall Street investment banker, watched the small white ball swing past the cup and roll to a halt some three feet beyond the flag. He'd been missing all day long, his concentration ragged, his coordination shot. Weighing the ball in his hand, he turned in the direction of the house. He could see his wife talking to the handyman, a kid called Peter Somebody she'd employed a couple of weeks ago. He wasn't a kid really, he was somewhere in his early thirties and wore his hair in a ponytail, the style that had been prevalent in the sixties. An old hippie, Huntington thought: the word hippie seemed peculiar these days. He tugged on the green eyeshade he wore, which, whether the sun was out or not, had become an integral part of his putting costume, like the white leather shoes, the red sweater, the gloves. He moved toward the next hole. His wife was still chatting with Peter; sometimes she'd reach out and touch the young man's arm to make a point.

Daniel put the ball down and looked through the trees. He couldn't concentrate today, no matter how hard he tried. He felt sluggish, lethargic, mocked by his own inability to knock a little white ball into a hole. He swung the putter gently, heard the satisfying click of metal against the ball, then saw the white object roll to the left of the flag. Closer than last time, but not good enough.

45

When he raised his face he saw his wife come across the green. Something in the way she moved always fascinated him: she walked as if she were conscious of an imaginary audience following her with its eyes. The word he always fumbled around was grace. Her long lemon dress skimmed the grass. Grace and power, he thought, although it was a kind of power Wall Street hadn't prepared him for.

"Winning, Danny?" she asked.

Nobody had ever called him Danny in his life. He'd never allowed it. Danny was a freckled boy in a soapbox derby, not a Wall Street banker. His wife, however, made the name sound desirable. He had been fifty-eight when he'd first met her, and like many people who have been unaccustomed to love's ways over a lifetime, he had been knocked sideways into an adolescence he'd managed to avoid the first time around. She introduced him to playfulness, simple joys, trifling things he'd never had time for before. He had retired, taken her on an extensive trip to the Far East, then to Australia and New Zealand, married her in Cape Town, brought her home and installed her in this house. The age difference between them, twenty-some years, had never troubled him.

"Winning isn't in the cards today," he said.

She watched him from the edge of the green. Some way behind her he could see Peter make something out of wood, he could hear the rasping sound of an electric saw. She moved toward him and slid her sunglasses up to the top of her head: there were pale circles under her eyes and he remembered how she'd been unable to sleep at night recently, and how even when she slept she'd been disturbed by dreams she could never remember on waking.

"It's a lonely game," she said.

Daniel nodded. He picked up his ball and rolled it around in the palm of his hand. Listening to the buzz of the electric saw, he wondered what the handyman was making over there; for a long time now he had wanted to do certain things to the house, paint it, refurbish it, even get rid of those ghastly statues his wife had bought. He'd always been puzzled by the grotesques: his personal taste in matters of art came to a stop at Maxfield Parrish. So he didn't understand the statues and he didn't grasp the reason for her purchase of them. One day, they had simply turned up, and he had never bothered to ask for an explanation.

He had ceased to ask for explanations when it came to his wife.

"Allow me," she said, taking the putter from his hand.

He watched her line up the ball, stand behind it, then strike it lightly; it ran around the rim of the cup, dangled there a moment, and finally dropped inside.

"Luck," he said, knowing that luck had little to do with her life; she was the kind of person who, through her own determination, created what passed as luck. He touched the back of her neck softly, watched her smile.

"Is that what you think?" she said.

"Not really." He went to the hole and retrieved the ball, then looked at her. He wasn't sure why he asked the question but it came out anyhow: "Are you happy?"

She pulled the sunglasses over her eyes again. "That's an odd question, Danny. Why do you ask?"

He shrugged. Why indeed? After a lifetime of asking other kinds of questions, questions of business, of acquisitions and bottom-line profits and financial projections, he was still somewhat puzzled by emotional inquiries. There was a whole dark continent inside himself that he hadn't had the time to explore.

"I don't know. You haven't seemed yourself lately." And he thought suddenly of that sad-faced little lawyer who had come, Leon Coldwind, and wondered if his question was bound up with Coldwind's recent visit.

"Perhaps I have things on my mind," she said.

"Is it anything you can share?"

"I don't think so, Danny. But thanks anyway."

"I'm always here," he said.

"I know you are and I appreciate it—" Something buzzed against the side of her face, a fly, a mosquito, and she swatted it away.

"Always," he said again.

Skyler was moving across the terrace, calling out her name. "Mrs. Huntington. Mrs. Huntington. Telephone. Telephone for you."

Daniel saw her go indoors. The house swallowed her, her disappearance into it was somehow final—a person casually drifting into a black hole. Then, even if he wasn't sure he wanted to, he walked around to the front of the house and paused before the statues. Why here, for God's sake? Why had she stuck the monstrosities here? And they frightened him.

There were four of them in all.

Four figures.

It was difficult to speculate about their sex.

All four appeared to be caught in the black core of a nightmare.

All four appeared to be shielding their faces from some horror.

Daniel Huntington closed his eyes for a second: they were too much; there was a quality about them that he could only think of as obscene. The sculptor must have fallen into the darkest places of his own psyche to have dredged up these horrors. If she had to have these figures, he thought, she might at least have put them indoors where they wouldn't have to be seen by anyone who arrived at the house.

He stared at the blank eyes, the open mouths, the twisted hands.

He looked at the way the faces ran into formless, asexual bodies.

And then he went down on one knee, examining the bases of the figures, where he saw—lightly carved—the initials of the sculptor.

SM.

Who had carved the bizarre little group that lingered around the entranceway as if they were figures frozen in the act of guarding the gateway to hell?

4

Gastopolous stood over their table, holding a page from the *Chronicle* in his hand. He was beaming and held the paper high as if he meant everybody in the restaurant to see it.

"I would kiss your hand, Kreesty, only I think your husband might object. We Greeks have poor reputations, undeserved I might say, but poor nevertheless. . . . I will content myself with thanking you for your article." And, somewhat comically, he bowed from the waist.

Christy watched him move from table to table, introducing himself to each diner. She looked at Zachary, who was studying the menu in a withdrawn fashion, as if he had no appetite, although it had been his suggestion when she'd picked him up at the station. A surprise, a pleasant one—it had been months since they'd last gone out to dinner together.

"What did you say to make him so happy?" he asked.

"I just mentioned his restaurant in my column—"

"It must have been glowing."

"I wasn't especially fulsome," she said. "I mentioned the ambience, the music . . ." She made a small indeterminate gesture with her hand: why was it so hard to divine his mood tonight? Maybe he'd had a lousy day at the office, maybe he hadn't been able to get a seat on the train.

Zachary put the menu down. "I need a drink," he said.

"How was your day anyway?"

"Middling. Yours?"

She hesitated a moment before she said, "I went for a drive. I stopped at The Falcon and had a drink."

"Alone?"

No, she wanted to say, I had the Bristol High School Marching Band and half the marine cadets from Shoreville with me and I managed to service them all between drinks. "Quite alone," she said. She wondered when a lie ceased to be small, or whether every lie was of the same magnitude, no matter the motive behind it. She was on the point of mentioning Richie, but what purpose would that serve?

A waiter came to their table with complimentary drinks, courtesy of the management. Two glasses of ouzo. She watched Zack sample his, then make a slight face.

"What are you going to eat?" she asked.

"I think the salad and the lamb kebab."

"Sounds good to me." She sipped her drink. The waiter took their order; Zachary became silent for a time, leaning back in his chair and studying the musicians.

Christy got up. "I'm going to wash my hands. Back in a moment."

She was conscious of Zachary watching her go across the room. She found the door marked REST ROOMS and pushed it open.

There was a long corridor in front of her. As she moved along it, looking for the ladies' room, she was aware of somebody standing inside the phone booth at the far end of the hallway.

51

A man.

He was turning to face her, smiling, already pushing the glass door of the booth open, already walking toward her.

She had a strange feeling suddenly.

Strange, unwanted.

Like she belonged to a conspiracy she'd entered inadvertently. *I don't need this. I don't need to feel that I'm meeting somebody behind Zachary's back even if it isn't true*—

"Christy," he said. "This is a real surprise."

"You're following me around, aren't you? I mean, none of this has been coincidental, has it? Am I right, Richie?"

"Why would I follow you?"

"I don't know."

"Think about it, Christy. What reason would I have for following you? I can't think of a single one. Can you?"

"Why are you here, Richie?"

"I was here yesterday, I liked the place, I like Greek food, I thought I'd come back again—"

Why wasn't she convinced by this? Why didn't this make sense to her?

She moved slightly away from him, as if she were afraid of getting too close. *Think it over, Christy. He hasn't made a pass at you. He hasn't suggested anything of an intimate nature. He hasn't been anything other than pleasant. So why would he follow you?* She had heard of harassment cases, guys obsessively stalking women, stalking and watching but never doing anything to harm them. *What if Richie turned out to be somebody like that?*

She stared into his face and for a moment she had the weird feeling that he was going to reach down and kiss her; and she understood, with a sinking sensation, that she would have yielded herself, she would have let him kiss her, she would have wanted that experience—no, no, no, it wasn't true, she didn't want any contact with him, this was just some simple aberration of the mind, a trick of the senses. It had something to do with the forced intimacy she suddenly felt, running into him in the corridor like this while all the time conscious of Zachary waiting at the table, unaware of this encounter. Yes, a forced intimacy, a sense of conspiracy again.

He isn't following me, she thought.

And I am not drawn to him.

"Okay," she said. "I believe you, Richie. I believe you."

He appeared enormously relieved. "I'm glad, Christy. Really glad. You've got to put more faith in good old coincidence, don't you?"

"I was never big on coincidences," she answered. "Because when they start to pile up, you begin to look for the pattern."

"And there isn't one."

She smiled at him and then she walked past him toward the bathroom. She ran her hands under the cold-water faucet and looked at her face in the mirror. The phantom kiss, she thought, and she wanted to laugh at herself—what had she given into just then? Some schoolgirlish conceit? Something she might have lifted off the pages of a romantic magazine. The kiss of the handsome stranger. Illicit Passion in Greek Restaurant. It had been a solitary foolish moment, and she wasn't going to think about it again. Sometimes your own brain could be the flophouse for some pretty low-rent notions.

The corridor was empty now; Richie had gone. She made her way back into the restaurant and she- wondered if

53

perhaps she looked different in some weird way, if Zachary could just gaze at her face and detect something. But this was nonsense too—there was nothing to detect.

She sat down, picked at her salad, pushed olives aside.

"I was going to send out a search party," he said. He smiled thinly.

She took his hand. Nothing had happened out there in that hallway. Nothing. It had been a mirage.

She put some lettuce in her mouth and found it tasteless.

"I love you," she said.

When he was sure that Christy was asleep, Zachary got out of bed and went downstairs. The only light in the lower part of the house was from the weak bulb that burned above the stove. He walked through the kitchen barefoot; inside the study he turned on a lamp and sat down behind his desk. Then he opened the center drawer of the desk and took out Leonora's letter. He studied the words awhile, and left a streak of sweat on the paper. Closing his eyes, he remembered—with a sense of deep regret—his clandestine meeting with Rucker in the park. Go back to the place where that started, he thought, go back and press the cancel key, obliterate the whole business. Trust Christy. If loving was trust, trust Christy.

His hand was shaking a little.

He listened to the silent house a moment, then reached out and picked up the telephone, dialing a number he didn't need to remember. It rang for a long time at the other end.

Leonora's voice.

"You do keep uncivilized hours, Zachary," she said.

"I wasn't going to call—"

"You received my letter? My telephone message? You

54

know, Zachary, you can't lie to me. When I called your office I knew instinctively that you were there at the time, no matter what your little secretary said. Am I right?"

"You're always right." He sighed quietly. He suddenly thought of Leonora as one might think of a large black spider sitting in the middle of a web, spinning and conniving, caught up in the intricate architecture of her creation.

"Your wife, Zachary. How is she?"

"She's very good for me—"

"Which is one kind of answer. Why wasn't I informed at the time? Why wasn't I invited to the wedding? Did you think you could avoid me?"

"It was a very quiet affair, Leonora."

"Christy. Christy. What kind of a name is that?"

"It's short for Christine—"

A pause. He heard Leonora laugh softly. "Will it last, Zachary?"

He didn't answer that question.

"When do I get to meet this Christy?"

"I . . ."

"You're faltering, Zachary. You're avoiding things. I don't exactly live on the other side of the world, do I? When I last looked at a map I noticed that you live in the next county."

"I don't think you should meet."

"Why not? Is there something you're afraid of? Is that it, Zachary?"

Afraid, yes, he thought—and suddenly he had the desire to lay his head in Leonora's lap and feel her hand stroke his hair, soothing him, consoling him, obliterating all the bruises, the business of just living.

"Are there things you haven't told her, Zachary? Is that it? Are you afraid of that?"

"I don't know," and he heard himself begin to stutter a little. "It's just that she's perfect for me, I couldn't believe anything might be this perfect ever—"

"Perfection, my dear, can be an illusion." Leonora sighed, then was quiet a moment. "So. When do I get to meet this paragon?"

"Please, Leonora . . ."

"I hardly think you can keep putting off the moment, Zachary. You're beginning to make me rather impatient."

Zachary felt himself tremble. He'd done so many things badly, he'd made mistakes—but when it came to Christy he wanted everything to be right. Perfection—why do I need to spoil perfection? He shut his eyes and imagined Rucker out there in his dark little world, the world of the gutter: what kind of man hires somebody like Rucker to spy on his own wife?

Reasons, Zachary.

You have reasons.

Bad reasons.

He opened his eyes and stared across the darkened room.

"I sometimes wonder if perhaps you forget how much I love you, Zachary," Leonora said. "I sometimes wonder if you underestimate my feelings, my dear. Tell me that it isn't true."

"I know how you feel, Leonora, I know how much you love me," and he felt stifled all at once, the air around him thick and cloying. "And you know my feelings."

There was a pause before Leonora said, "Perhaps better than you do yourself. Now I really must catch up on my sleep." She paused again. "Too much time has passed since we last met, Zachary, which is something I blame you for. We won't let it happen this way again, will we? Will we, Zachary?"

"No, Leonora. Of course not."

The connection was dead.

Zachary rose and went upstairs to the bedroom, walking in a weary way, like a man who has lost all feeling in his legs. He opened the bedroom door and looked at Christy.

She was asleep, beautiful even in sleep.

Perfection, he thought again.

How long could it last?

No: it had to last. He had to make it endure. More than anything else, he had to accomplish that.

A bad dream, a nightmare, something he had to push himself up from, thrusting his mind forward out of the depths of sleep, sweating, kicking the bedsheets away, raising his fists in the air, sitting upright with his eyes open.

He switched on the bedside lamp, blinked, rubbed his eyes. Clay, the dream had had something to do with clay, something frightening. He got out of bed and, shivering, moved into the bathroom. His head ached. He opened the medicine cabinet, found a tiny bottle of aspirin and swallowed two quickly, without water. He shut his eyes and leaned over the sink and had the feeling he was going to throw up. The muscles in his stomach hurt. Clay clay clay— what did the dream have to do with that?

He was cold. He went back inside the bedroom and found his robe, draped it over his shoulders, walked to the window. He remembered the Greek restaurant—she'd been surprised by his appearance, very surprised; and there had been something else as well, a shiver that he'd felt, as if cold electricity were passing between them, deep vibrations. He knew that she had felt it too.

It wasn't going to take much longer now.

He knew this with certainty.

And then he was thinking of the dream again. Christy had been involved, though he wasn't sure how. Christy and something to do with clay—

Wrong wrong wrong.

Not clay. Marble.

Yes, marble.

Now he remembered, but the memory was painful to him, like something inside a box whose lid had sprung open. A box he needed to close.

Close it, he said to himself.

Close it right now.

5

Christy liked The Dying Swan. It was a small bar filled with enough potted plants to afford a pleasing sense of camouflage. After a day's work she would sometimes come here to kill a little time before she had to pick up Zachary at the station.

She ordered her usual Scotch and soda, lit a cigarette and stared through the leaves of plants at the street. A glorious fall day, the afternoon sun red and warm, a few dead leaves already shuffling along the sidewalks. She looked at her watch. 4:29. Today she'd covered the Nurses' Auxiliary Charity Book Sale and a reception at St. Matthew's Hospital for some visiting surgeon; now she took her notebook from her purse and flicked the pages, looking at her own unusual shorthand.

She'd never taken any courses in journalism in college. Back then, she'd been more interested in the idea of writing a book, and she had started novels on more than one occasion—none of them had ever grown to the point where she knew she was compelled to finish them. That's what she had lacked, she thought: a sense of compulsion. So she had turned to journalism, working on a small newspaper in the boondocks of Vermont, learning everything at a furious rate, keenly aware of the fact that she hadn't had the training of her colleagues. When the chance to work on the *Bristol Chronicle* had come up, she'd grabbed it. The social column had been given to her on her first day and she'd written it ever since, a matter of some two years. Despite Rossiter's ambitions for her, she imagined she'd go on writing it . . . until . . .

Until what?

Until Zachary decided they should start a family?

She pushed her notebook aside, sipped her drink.

Kids, she thought. Zachary had problems of his own, without having to take on those of a family. And she considered how he had behaved during the last couple of days, at times unreachable, drifting away into silences she couldn't fathom. Was it his work? Did he have problems with his company? He'd never mentioned any—in fact, he never offered any kind of explanation for his moods: he was sometimes like a stranger, a perception that made her feel suddenly very chill.

Like a stranger—what an awful perception about your own husband. About the man you loved.

She looked at the row of small storefronts that faced her. This was an old section of Bristol, crooked frame houses and narrow streets and quaint little shops. But it wasn't the shops she was studying now. She held her breath.

Richie was standing on the sidewalk opposite.

She watched him cross the street. He knows where I am. He knows where I go. Why does he seem to know so much about my life?

She felt very vulnerable.

You can't keep on toying with the notion of coincidence. It's beyond that now. Coincidence was not enough to explain these encounters.

She took a pair of sunglasses out of her purse and put them on, and then thought how ludicrous it was to try to hide from him.

She knew without looking that he was coming toward her table.

He sat down and stared at her for a long time without speaking.

"I'm not buying it this time, Richie," she said.

"Not buying what?"

"That this is sheer coincidence—"

He placed one hand directly over his heart. "I confess. I own up. I was passing the *Chronicle* building when I saw you leave. I called out your name a couple of times, but I guess you didn't hear me."

Passing the *Chronicle* building. Just happened to be passing it. Okay. Consider the plausibility of that one. Where does it take you? She shook her head. "Why are you following me, Richie?"

"I have a sense of déjà vu," he answered, smiling.

That smile—it was all charm, all ease and poise and confidence. She said, "Frankly, I'm beginning to wonder, Richie. I'm beginning to wonder if there isn't some purpose to your surprise appearances."

He tapped his long, elegant fingers on the surface of the table. "Maybe I enjoy your company, Christy," he said eventually. "Maybe it's as simple as that. Perhaps I'm lonely."

"You? Lonely? I find that hard to believe—"

"Why? Certain people have difficulty in finding new friends, and I might be one of them."

61

"So you think I can be your friend, is that it?"

"Why not?" He looked at her appealingly.

"Well, for one thing, I think you might be going the wrong way about it, Richie. Put yourself in my position—how would you feel about somebody following you around?"

"I never said I was following you, Christy. Did I?"

She was silent. She had a sense of something shifting here, an enigma, as if Richie's center were forever changing, so that you could not quite get to the heart of the man. Okay, he wanted to be friends, but where was that going to lead? How would friendship satisfy him? Then she was thinking of Zachary; the landscape of her husband seemed strewn with mines, any one of which could explode. What would he say if you brought Richie home and introduced him as your new friend?

She looked at his face, remembering the moment in the Greek restaurant—and suddenly she felt fear: the idea of being followed, of having her movements read as if they were lines in an open book, her privacy interrupted, these things unsettled her.

"Smile," he said.

"What?"

"Smile. You look better when you don't frown."

She forced her lips apart in a grimace.

"Very disappointing," he said.

"I don't feel like smiling right now. You worry me, Richie. Can't you see that you place me in a difficult situation?"

"Why?"

"I'm married—" What was she saying? Was she openly admitting the possibility of a romantic involvement? An affair? She hadn't meant to sound that way at all; she had only wanted to make it clear that a married woman wasn't always in the position to make friends with an attractive man.

And then—

He lowered his hand, covering hers.

"Don't do that," she said.

"Then you have the option of taking your hand away—"

Childish. Absurd. "My hand was here first, Richie."

He started to laugh and after a moment she joined him and then she realized her hand was still buried beneath his, a connection of flesh that embarrassed her.

"Richie, please."

He sat back in his chair, his hands in his pockets now.

"Richie, I'm not looking for a relationship, can't you see that? I'm not looking for something that could get tricky, I'm not searching like some bored suburban housewife prowling shopping malls in the afternoons, studying the shapes of boys in supermarkets, I'm not like that—"

"What are you like, Christy?"

"Goddammit," she said. "I don't think you listen to me, do you?"

"I think we could get to know each other a little better, that's all," he said.

"And what does that mean?" She thought: I should get up right now, walk away from here . . .

Instead of answering her, he stood up, still smiling.

He took something from his pocket.

Something metallic attached to a plastic tag. He dropped it on the table.

And then, saying nothing, he walked out of the bar.

She reached for the object. It was a key to a room in the

63

Concorde Hotel. She picked it up and turned it over and over in the palm of her hand. This is the place where it stops, she thought. This is the line you have to draw now.

She could see him crossing the street, looking back once before he disappeared around a corner—a slender, good-looking young man who walked with the grace of an athlete.

And she studied the key. There was temptation, she had to admit that much. There was temptation to pick up the key and, as if it were a gauntlet he had thrown down, a dare he had offered, take it to the hotel and let herself into his room, and there—

But this was fantasyland again, this was the place for soft-core dreams, idle moments of the heart. This was a world that was safe to visit only inside her head.

It's flattering that he wants me to go to his hotel room and get into bed with him. But this goes no further now. This ends right here.

She tossed the key aside and looked out through the window at the empty street.

Zachary stepped off the train, expecting to see Christy waiting for him, but the platform was deserted. He walked toward the gate, looking this way and that, seeing nothing; then he was standing at the edge of the parking lot.

No Jaguar.

No Christy.

He turned and strolled back. Something has happened to her, he thought, something has made her late. A simple delay, maybe a sudden deadline. He stared at the rails for a moment, following them with his gaze to the point where they vanished inside the darkness of a tunnel. There was a cold edge to the evening. He tucked his hands inside the pockets of his overcoat, his briefcase against his side. She had never been late before.

A porter walked past, glancing at him a moment.

Zachary moved a little way along the platform; then he was back at the edge of the parking lot again. Five or six cars: no maroon Jag.

Where is she? Right at this moment, where is she? A nerve moved beneath his eye and he rubbed the place but the tic wouldn't go away. He leaned against the fence. Consider: she's been in an accident. She's lying now in a hospital bed. She's badly hurt. Or worse.

Please come, he thought.

And just as he wished it, the Jaguar came into the parking lot and Christy was calling out to him through the open window.

"I know, I know, I'm late, I'm sorry . . ."

He got in on the passenger side and touched her face delicately, almost as if he doubted her physical presence.

"I'm useless in waiting situations," he said. "I never know what to do, what to think . . . I'm prone to panic." He realized he was trying to sound lighthearted to make nothing out of her lateness.

"The traffic was bad downtown. There was an accident right at the corner of Tenth and Central, you know how that can back everything up for hours. I'm sorry if you panicked." She was speaking breathlessly, quickly, as if she'd been running rather than driving a car.

"The panic hadn't quite congealed," he said. An accident, he thought. What if I ask her to take me to the scene, what if I say I'm interested in looking at this collision? And then he despised himself for this sudden upsurge of his own doubts. He leaned toward her and kissed the side of her face. I am a ridiculous person. Impaled upon my own fears. Perhaps one day I will find the strength to make them disappear.

She said, "I'll take the back roads home."

"Sounds like a good idea." He pulled his briefcase onto his lap. "Tell me about your day . . ."

"Busy busy busy. A reception at St. Matthew's and some nurses' charity affair. All the important stuff," and she turned to smile at him; he felt a slight dismay as she did so because he caught the unmistakable scent of alcohol on her breath. Tell me where you had the drink, Christy. It was simple, she stopped somewhere along the way, she went into a bar, perhaps, or maybe they served booze at St. Matthew's.

"I had a terrible day," he said.

"I'm sorry . . ."

"They happen every so often. Things slide, they get out of control, you can't make repairs. The funny thing is, I kept getting this feeling that the worst was still to come."

Christy looked sympathetic. "We'll have a quiet night at home. I'll cook us something nice. We'll open some wine."

"Spoil me," he said. "I feel I deserve it."

Christy turned the Jaguar onto a narrow side road and their house came into sight. She steered toward the gravel drive.

There was something Zachary always found very satisfying about the way tires crunched, but not now, not now. He leaned forward in his seat, chilled, a sudden quickening of ice in his blood.

"Look," Christy said, pointing toward the house.

A car, a long black limousine, sat in the driveway.

"Do you know that car, Zach?"

He didn't say anything, conscious of his hands gripping the briefcase.

"Is it anybody we know?"

"Yes," he replied in a whisper.

He stepped out of the Jaguar and stared at the Cadillac. A rear window was rolled down. He found himself looking at Leonora. He fought against the sensation of things slipping inside him, tumbling and breaking, and then he smiled and looked at Christy, who had emerged from the Jaguar and was staring at Leonora in a puzzled way.

"Christy, I'd like you to meet—" Zachary paused; his mouth was dry. *I don't want her here, I don't need her, I don't need the overflow of her life into mine, and I don't need any of the consequences she always brings.* And he realized how scared he felt, how much he had dreaded this intrusion and what it might cause.

"I'd like you to meet my sister, Leonora."

"Shall we go inside?" Leonora asked, as if the house were hers.

She hadn't come.

It was a simple fact but he couldn't entirely deal with it.

It seemed to rattle around inside his head like a loose marble, knocking, ricocheting.

He had given her the key but she hadn't come.

He beat his hands together in frustration, walking up and down the room, feeling energy burn up inside. After the situation in the bar he'd felt very confident, certain she'd turn up at the hotel in a short time, positive she'd rush to be with him. Totally sure.

But now . . .

He sat on the bed. He clenched his hands together.

The room oppressed him. He had to get out, get his car, drive somewhere, anywhere.

He didn't move for a time.

Paralysis. A weakening of his confidence.

Somebody went along the corridor outside, and for a second he imagined . . . But the footsteps faded away.

He rose, went inside the bathroom, looked at himself in the mirror as if he might see some reason for failure in his face. Lines, wrinkles, marks that might threaten his appearance. Nothing. He pulled his lips back and examined his teeth. White, straight, perfect.

What then?

He moved back into the bedroom and strolled to the window, watching traffic moving along the street. She would come round. They always did. She was playing a little game with him, nothing more. That was it—a little game. He smiled to himself; he was getting upset over nothing at all.

She had the key.

It was only a matter of time.

"I rather like the way you have this study, Christine," Leonora was saying. As she spoke she moved her fingers ever so slightly in her lap. She might have been stroking an invisible cat, Christy thought.

"Call me Christy . . ."

"Christy," and Leonora seemed to turn the word over inside her mouth, as though it were something she couldn't quite swallow.

"My parents always called me Christy. Never Christine . . ." Christy heard herself laugh; she wasn't sure why. Nerves, kid, a sudden attack of nerves: she couldn't bring herself to look at Zachary, who was hovering on the edges of the room and looking miserable.

"Tell me about your family, dear," Leonora said.

"My parents are both dead. I never had any brothers or sisters. My father was in timber . . . ."

"Timber?"

Christy nodded. She looked at Leonora in her black clothes and a simple onyx necklace that trapped the light and seemed to freeze it. A sister-in-law, Christy thought, a sister by marriage—suddenly you find you have a relative you never knew about. She wondered if Zachary had others hidden away somewhere. All kinds of brothers and sisters tucked away in closets and attics. She glanced at her husband: you and I have something to discuss, sweetheart.

"Is there money in timber?" Leonora asked.

"He made a comfortable living."

"And how did he die?"

"Suddenly. A heart attack."

"How terrible for you." Leonora looked toward Zachary, smiling at him. "Fetch me a drink, Zachary. Something alcoholic with a twist of lemon. It doesn't matter what."

Zachary wandered away, like a large dog sent to do his mistress's bidding. He responds to her without question, Christy thought, as if he were glad of an excuse to leave the room. His discomfort was almost palpable, an electric current in the study. And that's what he should feel: complete discomfort.

Leonora opened her purse and took out a cigarette. The black dress, black purse, black shoes—the woman created a core of darkness at the center of the room, and yet she occupied the space on the sofa quite naturally, with great ease, like someone accustomed to authority, to deferential treatment.

"It's a blow to lose both parents," Leonora said. "Our own parents died when we were very young." She blew a fine stream of smoke upward, like strands of a delicate web.

"Zack's never said very much about his family."

"Is that so?"

Christy nodded, conscious of Zachary coming back into the room with drinks, hearing ice rattle inside glasses. Zack has never said a goddamn thing about his family, she thought. Nothing, as if his whole history was a sweet zero; he'd arrived in the world by artificial insemination. Later, when Leonora has gone, we'll talk this whole thing over. She felt betrayed by her husband now, by the concealment of a sister: it was a mystery and she'd stumbled into it without Zack's help. Why didn't you ever mention a sister to me, Zachary?

"Zachary has always been reticent," Leonora said, taking her drink from him—and something passed between them, a look, a sign, a collusion of eyes that Christy couldn't quite read. "Haven't you, dear?"

"I suppose," Zachary said, turning toward Christy with a glass of Scotch and soda, which she took without looking at him. She became aware of Zachary melting away again, vanishing into a corner like a child banished from adult company. A naughty boy.

"Are there others?" Christy asked. "Brothers? Sisters?"

Leonora shook her head. She tasted her drink. "Zachary, you've been miserly with the lemon, haven't you?" She smiled in her brother's direction.

"I'll fix it," he started to say.

"It's fine. It's palatable."

70

A silence. And then Leonora stubbed her cigarette in an ashtray. She moved with a fluidity that was intriguing to watch, like someone who has spent years dancing, training her muscles. But there was a suggestion of strain in her face, something that had nothing to do with muscle control, as if she were keeping something bound up inside, something very tight.

"When he was a small boy, Zachary could never do anything right. I remember I used to ask him to make tea or coffee, or fetch me something to drink, and he'd never get it right. His tea always turned out like dishwater and his coffee like a very weak soup." Leonora laughed to herself.

Christy wondered if Zachary had spent his whole childhood fetching things for his sister.

"It's a pleasant house. It feels like a home," Leonora said.

"I'm glad you think so," said Christy.

"You must come and visit me sometime. I don't live very far from here. Zachary knows where the house is."

Does he? Christy thought. What else does he know?

And then something curious happened. Leonora walked across the room and knelt on the rug at Christy's feet. She stared, scrutinizing Christy's face, her dark eyes searching for something. Uncomfortable, Christy smiled, a smile that froze on her face when she felt Leonora's hand go under her chin.

"There's some resemblance," Leonora whispered.

"What resemblance? I don't think I follow you—"

Zachary's voice was harsh: "There's none, Leonora. You're imagining things, that's all."

Leonora stood up now. "Yes, yes, I suppose I am . . ."

Christy looked from one to the other. What the hell kind of game is this? Who am I supposed to look like?

71

"I'm sorry," Leonora said. "It was a mistake."

"I don't get this, any of it. Who am I supposed to resemble?"

They were both silent, in the manner of people who have conspired together to ignore any questions that might erode their conspiracy; brother and sister, she thought, bound by blood, by blood secrets.

"Let's not discuss it," Leonora said. "A simple error on my part."

No, Christy thought, it wasn't a mistake, it was deliberate.

Leonora picked up her purse, glanced at her watch. "I'm sorry I have to run along. I wish I could stay longer, Christy. I hope Zachary will bring you to my house soon. You'll do that, won't you, Zachary?"

Zachary nodded. Leonora was moving toward the door and Christy followed her out into the hallway.

"My driver is probably asleep," Leonora said. "He's very old and rather afraid of modern traffic problems, but he's loyal, and loyalty is something of a prize these days, don't you agree?"

She reached out and kissed Christy on the cheek. A peck, a quick, formal peck. Then she stepped out into the night, turning at the edge of the steps to smile one last time.

"I think I prefer you to Anthea, Christy. Yes, I think I do. I think we can be good friends."

And then she was gone, walking toward the driver who was already getting out and opening the back door for her.

Christy watched the car move along the gravel driveway.

Anthea, she thought.

Anthea and resemblances.

A sister who turns up out of nowhere, out of lies, out of omissions, out of the dust.

* * *

Daniel Huntington listened to the sound of his wife climbing the stairs. He turned over in bed and, through the open bedroom doorway, saw her shadow against the wall. When it had gone he closed his eyes because he felt a kind of weary impotence. He had been waiting for her with anticipation, looking forward to the sight of her undressing in the bedroom, the eggshell luster of her skin, her small rounded breasts and smooth long legs. The anticipation had seemed to him like an exotic taste in his mouth. Waiting, waiting for love. Waiting for the feel of her body, the touch of her lips, the sight of her fingers exploring him: waiting for that moment when he thought his heart might explode and he would experience a brief apocalyptic joy.

Nothing.

He got out of bed quickly and went to the foot of the stairs to call up after her. From the upper part of the house he could hear her footsteps stop.

"Is something wrong?" he asked. A vague teasing echo rang from the depths of the house.

She didn't answer him at once. He imagined her up there, leaning against the rail, isolated from him by something more than a flight of stairs. Don't go, he thought. Come back down here, be with me.

"Darling, if something's wrong, why don't you come down here and we can talk about it?" That damned echo. He put his hand out to the rail, clutched it, and peered up into the shadows for a sight of her, but the angle of stairs made it impossible. The silence that followed his question made him feel she had vanished someplace above him, that he'd never find her again even if he searched this large house for the rest of his life.

73

And then her voice, quiet, small: "I need to think . . ."

"Please, I'd like to see you."

No answer.

"Please," he heard himself whisper.

There was only the sound of her footsteps again as she moved toward the next flight. He started to climb after her. What was wrong with her? Why did she have to hide herself away like this?

Sweating, he reached the landing.

He stopped, staring toward the stairs.

Overhead, there was the sound of a door clicking shut.

Her room, her damned room.

He had known that was where she was going, he had known from the first moment of hearing her go up. That little room at the top of the house, her private space.

Some time ago, she had told him she needed a place where she could go when she wanted to be alone, when she had to have peace to think things over. He remembered how easily he had acquiesced, because that was what he always did, but now—now he wished he had been a little more authoritative, less yielding.

What kinds of things did she need to think over anyhow?

At first he imagined that perhaps she needed a place where she could get away from him, but he found this thought so unsettling that he refused to countenance it. Now, as he climbed toward the closed door, thinking about her changes in mood and her need for solitude, thinking about these strictly human mysteries, he realized he'd never gone inside the room, didn't know what she had in there, had no idea of the nature of the place or how she passed her time. Another kind of man, he reflected, would simply break down the door. Another kind of man, not me.

He stopped outside, listened, his head tilted at an angle.

He could hear nothing. Only the rushing silences of the house.

He raised his hand as if to knock; but he couldn't even bring himself to do that. You wanted her in bed tonight. You wanted her close to you. He shut his eyes and could feel the sweat roll over the surface of his body.

Why does she need this room? Why?

He pressed his face against the wood and whispered, "Good night. Good night, Leonora."

There was no answer.

6

Humiliated.

No, it was more than that.

It was more than that she felt.

She clenched her hands in the pockets of her jacket and turned to look back at the house from the lawn, where she stood with Zachary, and she could still feel Leonora's presence as surely as if the woman were silhouetted against one of the windows.

Leonora.

A card pulled out of some dusty old pack.

Leonora. Anthea.

And the night all around her seemed filled with whispers, as if those two names were being uttered quietly from the dark places between the trees.

She could hardly bring herself to look at Zachary. Afraid that if she did she wouldn't see the face of the man she'd married, the man whose quiet strengths and tenderness had first drawn her to him. Afraid she'd see something altogether different.

A stranger's mask.

And then it was like a bad dream in which you're walking along a moonlit country road with a person you think you can trust more than anyone else in the whole world and when you turn to look you suddenly see a transformation, you see a familiar face melt like wax, you see a monster.

Without looking at him she said, "Start at the beginning."

Zachary smiled in an apologetic way. "I don't know why I never told you about Leonora before."

"Love, you're going to have to do better than that," she said. She walked some little distance away from him now, further into the trees. "We took certain marriage vows, I recall—" She turned to face him: the wedding, she was suddenly thinking about the wedding and the absence of his relatives from the event—she thought he was an only child. It had been a quiet wedding attended only by a couple of his authors, a few of her old friends (that vanishing species) and Rossiter from the *Chronicle*.

Zachary moved toward her: "She and I don't get along, Christy. We never did mean that much to each other, I saw no point in mentioning her to you. I never thought she'd just show up like that."

It's weak, Christy thought. It's not altogether convincing. Even if he and Leonora had hated each other, surely he would have mentioned her name somewhere along the way, dropped it even by accident. But he never had. "I don't buy it," she said. "It didn't seem to me that you were out-and-out foes or anything like that—"

"Foes?" Zachary laughed. "Leonora and I aren't enemies."

"Know what I feel, Zack? I feel cheated, that's what. You're my husband, we're not supposed to have secrets

77

from one another, are we?" And she found herself turning the thought of Richie over in her mind. But what was that? Did that constitute some dark secret? Hardly. Richie meant nothing: she'd done nothing to encourage the man or his vague obsession with her, if that's what you could call it.

"I didn't mean anything harmful, you have to believe that," Zachary said.

She was silent. There was a pained look on his face, like that of a kid who has seen his misdeeds uncovered and now expects punishment. She looked upward through dark branches, recalling the way Leonora had studied her face, how she'd spoken about a resemblance. To whom? To Anthea? But somehow Christy didn't want to mention Anthea right now, afraid of what she might discover. A name out of nowhere. A name, a sequence of sounds. What have I got to be afraid of anyhow? she wondered. Anthea. She moved alongside Zachary, reaching out to touch the side of his face.

"What was all that other stuff about?" she asked.

"What stuff?"

"This person she said I looked like—"

"She made a mistake, that's all—"

A mistake: it had seemed more deliberate than that.

"Is it Anthea? Is that the person I look like?"

"Anthea?" He stared at her. Something hard in the expression, hard, distant. "Where did you hear that name?"

"Leonora mentioned it as she was leaving. She said she liked me more than Anthea." Zachary looked miserable. "An old girlfriend?" Christy continued. "Is that it? A name from your past?"

He said nothing. His past, she thought. She'd gone into the marriage knowing nothing of his past, but somehow

78

assuming there was nothing to know. But maybe his insecurities could be explained if there had been a girl in his history, if something painful had happened to him in another relationship.

"Anthea . . ." He stuttered slightly, catching his tongue on the name. It was something she'd never heard him do before.

"What is it, Zack?"

"Why did she bring that name up?"

"Hey, listen, you can tell me, you know that." And she stroked his arm: he was trembling. "Whatever it is, you can tell me—" But then she wasn't sure, because the expression on his face was one of withdrawal, as if Anthea were a name he never wanted to encounter again.

"Come on, Zack. Try. I'm listening."

He didn't speak.

"Zack, please. Whatever it is, I can handle it."

He lowered his face against her shoulder and she could feel it—his pain, his great reluctance to talk about the mystery of Anthea. She caught the back of his head in her hands and stroked his hair.

"Tell me. Go ahead."

He raised his face and tried to smile, but it wasn't a very good effort.

"Anthea," he said.

She waited: tense, she waited for him to speak.

She wasn't sure if she really wanted to hear what he had to say.

"Anthea was a very unhappy person, Christy. I used to think she'd been born that way. I used to think that she could find unhappiness in almost anything. Some people do."

79

It's coming, she thought.

And I don't want to know.

"The world was a black place for her. For everything good that happened there was always something bad. Sometimes, she wouldn't talk for days, she'd just lie in bed and stare at the ceiling, saying nothing."

Who? Christy wondered.

Tell me who she was.

Tell me what she meant to you.

And tell me what happened.

Zachary raised his face.

"I'm still listening, Zack."

"She's dead, Christy. I don't want to talk about her."

"Another goddamn secret? Is that it?"

He shook his head. "She's dead. There's nothing more to say."

"Like hell. You can't just bring up some name from your past and let it go like that."

Zachary turned away and began to walk back in the direction of the house. When she'd caught up, she seized his arm and tried to spin him around, but he shrugged her aside and kept walking.

She stood very still. "Zack, I'm warning you. I'm not going back inside that house with you until you tell me who this person was!"

Zachary stopped. He looked at her.

"Why do you need to know?"

"I need to know, that's all. Wouldn't you?"

He smiled a half smile, an uncertain expression.

"Maybe I would," he said.

"You're damn right you would," and she heard her own voice, a mad sound, echo through the dark trees. She thought: This is unreal, this conversation, the darkness around us, the whole thing.

"Anthea was my wife. Before you, I was married to Anthea."

She heard a ringing in her ears, as if her face had been struck, and struck very hard. She watched him reach the doorway and go inside, and then there was the sound of the door slamming shut.

The author, a broad-chested man with a face that had been subjected to too many violent suns in too many violent deserts, was explaining a theory he had begun to entertain during the past twelve years and about which he wanted to write a book—a book he thought would become an instant best-seller. The author's agent, who sat alongside him, was a leathery little woman in a floppy hat who had once known John Dos Passos and F. Scott Fitzgerald at a time when they had not been household names.

I am not listening, Zachary thought.

I am tuning these people out.

He tilted himself back in his chair and looked from the window into Forty-second Street and wished himself a thousand miles from this place. He'd been sick on the morning train, rushing to the rest room and holding his face over the toilet, bringing up nothing from his stomach. And now he was obliged to sit and listen to a man who held the theory that a race of superbeings inhabited the center of the earth.

"It could grab the Von Daniken market," the agent said. "And we know how big that one is. Besides, a number of rather respectable people have given serious consideration to Brad's theory."

The author concurred. Zachary fingered the slim outline that lay on his desk and wondered about woodwork and how many lunatics were getting prepared to crawl out of it. He heard himself say that he'd need time to think it over and then he was showing the pair out of his office, closing the door with relief and remembering how many odd projects he had been subjected to in recent years—that Hitler was a superintendent in a building in the Bronx, that Christ had returned in the person of one Samuel Sloan of White Plains. The list was insanely long.

He walked over to the window, rubbing the palms of his hands on his thighs. He wasn't thinking about the author and his agent now, he was remembering the train again, the feeling of nausea that had coursed through him, the way a manuscript had slipped from his fingers to the floor, a dizziness that had made his head spin as if from too many glasses of Scotch. Last night, last night with Christy . . .

Anthea.

He put his hand to his forehead. The telephone rang on his desk but he didn't bother to pick it up.

He shut his eyes and pressed his knuckles hard against his eyelids.

You take a faltering step back because Leonora comes with a dead woman's name on her lips.

He looked at the book jackets on the office walls and saw how they seemed to blur one into the other, the colors running like cheap dyes.

Last night with Christy had been painful, more than painful, dredging up things he imagined he'd managed to put away and keep locked, finding dark shadows from the past spilling out into the present—because of Leonora, because of her . . . He wished he could be down in the street right now, lost in the throng that crowded the sidewalk, one anonymous figure among so many.

Anthea. He didn't want to remember her. The past should be bound and padlocked and thrown into some deep ocean and left to rot among the silt on the black sea floor. Why was it so damned hard to be free of it?

He moved back to his desk. You think of Anthea, you let the image take root inside you, then suddenly you're back on the train again, feeling sick and dizzy . . .

A young woman is dead.

Leave it there.

He sat down, but pictures crowded him all at once, Anthea lying in bed and staring at the ceiling and retreating into that silent place where she felt most at home; pale, thin Anthea sitting in her big velvet chair at the window and staring wistfully out across the dark for the lover who ceased to appear; Anthea talking to herself in a crazy monotone, hands restless in her narrow lap.

No longer able to tolerate the confines of his office, he stepped out into the reception room, where the secretary, a tall girl with red hair and broad shoulders, smiled at him.

"Going out, Mr. McNair?"

He nodded, then said: "I'll be an hour. Maybe longer."

And then he was inside the elevator and traveling to the ground floor.

In Central Park Rucker was waiting for him on the same bench where they'd met before.

Zachary paused, looking at the fat man through the trees, watching him as he stared at a newspaper he clearly wasn't reading. Maybe it was a trick you had to acquire in Rucker's business, a gambit you had to know—the art of pretending one thing while you're doing quite another. As if he were blessed with peripheral vision, Rucker smiled even before he turned his face to look at Zachary.

Zachary said nothing; he sat down on the bench.

Rucker folded his newspaper: "Good to see you again, Mr. McNair."

"Likewise," Zachary said.

Rucker spread his big hands, then took an envelope from inside his coat—an envelope Zachary glanced at, feeling a moment of fear, a rush of anxiety.

"Field reports, Mr. McNair. On the subject of your wife. You want to read them? Or do you want me to give you the gist?"

"I don't need details," Zachary said. "The broad outline will do."

Rucker took some sheets of paper from the envelope; they were crisp and neatly typed and the paper was obviously expensive. He passed a hand over them in the fashion of a conjurer summoning silk ribbons from a hat and then he cleared his throat. "Our man in Bristol—"

"What man in Bristol?" Zachary said.

"Name's Thompson, a very good man, highly experienced . . ."

"I imagined that you would be doing this work yourself, Mr. Rucker—"

"Since I'm based here in Manhattan, that would be awkward, Mr. McNair. I can assure you, though, that Thompson is highly qualified . . ."

Zachary glanced at the papers. It was like throwing a stone into water, watching ripples grow wider and wider: he felt a little displeased that somebody else—this person Thompson—was involved in such a confidential matter.

"Anyhow, as I was saying—" Rucker peeled the pages:

"—there's hardly anything to report except for one small incident."

One small incident, Zachary thought. His fingernails dug into the palms of his hands. He realized he didn't want to hear anything bad about Christy: that he was looking to Rucker and his associates to give her a clean bill of health.

"She went to a bar called The Dying Swan."

"She stops there sometimes for a drink," Zachary said.

"Yeah. Well, on this occasion she was joined by a man—"

"A man?"

"A man. Young. Caucasian. Handsome. Well dressed."

A catalog of attributes. What happened? What happened in The Dying Swan?

"The man sat down at her table. According to Thompson this man and Mrs. McNair appeared to be at least superficially acquainted. They drank Scotches and then the man left. Mrs. McNair left shortly afterward."

"Did she join this man?"

"No," Rucker said. "She went to the station to pick you up."

"And the man? Did your Mr. Thompson manage to identify the man?"

Rucker shook his head. "Not yet."

There was a pain inside Zachary's head. It had the intensity of a slow fire, flame licking around his skull, penetrating the tender tissue. He moaned to himself and looked away from Rucker. A group of small kids was walking along the pathway, led by a middle-aged schoolteacher in a sweatsuit. The innocence of kids, he thought, trying to drive the idea of Christy's stranger out of his mind. Trying to silence the burning pain he was feeling.

A man.

A stranger.

They have a drink together.

She leaves. Picks me up at the station.

Why didn't she ever say anything about this man?

"Are you okay?" Rucker asked.

"I'm fine, just fine."

Rucker took out a handkerchief and blew his red nose. "Sometimes we discover unpleasant things, Mr. McNair. But Thompson hasn't been able to uncover any indication of impropriety on your wife's part."

Zachary stared across the park. Indication of impropriety. The salve of words. He got up from the bench and looked down at Rucker.

"Keep in touch," he said.

"Sure thing." Rucker didn't get up; Zachary turned and walked away.

The headache raged. On Fifth Avenue he stopped and leaned against the wall of a store. A man a man a man . . . what did it mean? Let it be something shallow, something innocent, a casual coincidence. Let it be ordinary, explicable.

Let it be something different from the last time.

All night long Christy had lain beside Zachary, caught up in a circle of sleeplessness, gazing at the moon against the window and wondering about the man who slept so restlessly at her side; she hadn't fallen asleep until the first streaks of light in the sky, and when she did her dreams were filled with haunting images, images—she supposed— of the enigmatic Anthea, a frail woman who was always one taunting step in front of her in the course of the dreams.

When she'd wakened from this inconclusive dreaming, Zachary had already gone. The bed was empty and the room filled with a hard autumnal sunlight, the kind of light in which everything seems starkly revealed. She felt weary as she drank her coffee and wearier still when she looked at her calendar for the day: an art gallery—the opening of something called the Gallery Marguerite, an event she didn't look forward to with very much enthusiasm because Bristol's art crowd was largely a matter of small-minded cliques with the delicacy of barracudas.

She dressed slowly, drank a second cup of coffee, then went inside the bathroom to apply some makeup. Her face in the mirror seemed paler than usual and beneath her eyes there were areas of darkness: she thought she looked like one of those shrunken heads that people used to purchase as souvenirs of trips to South America.

She walked out toward her car and yawned as she slid onto the seat. She glanced once at her image in the rearview mirror, made a face, then started the car and drove through Bristol, seeing the houses seemingly suspended in midair, poised on invisible stilts, streets running into the harsh light as if they were melting away, windows catching fire. An alien city, she thought—no, Christy, it's just you who feels alienated from things around you this morning because it isn't every day a woman learns that her husband has been married before, it isn't exactly a commonplace occurrence to find out that your husband has concealed his past to this extent, is it? Zachary's little secret; it was like he had a trapdoor in his life and you just happened to take a tumble through it, sweetie. Anthea McNair: that would have been her name.

Belatedly she stopped at a red light, hardly aware of the

traffic around her. And what precisely had happened to the late Mrs. McNair anyhow? What had caused her death? Zachary hadn't said; he'd taken the low road to some retreat of his own, hiding in his restless sleep, leaving her questions unanswered. Poor Anthea, whoever you are . . .

She watched the signal change and drove until she came to a narrow street in the old part of Bristol, a street of chic little stores and galleries and tourist traps, where everything was five times as expensive as anyplace else. She parked— very badly—and walked until she came to the Gallery Marguerite. I can't go inside, she thought, beset by a sense of panic. I can't go in there and smile and ask bright questions and pretend my whole world is perfectly in order. That had been yesterday, she thought: yesterday I had control.

She moved toward the door. A babble of conversation filled the air. His old love, his first wife—why had he never even mentioned the fact? This was what hurt her, dismayed her, his wall of silence. Did he think he could hide it forever? She tried to imagine Zachary with Anthea: a couple with linked arms and smiles of love, their eyes bright with the potential of the future; Zachary lying in bed with his first wife; Zachary and Anthea setting up house (Where? she wondered. Where the hell had he lived with her?); Zachary and Mrs. McNair settling down to evenings of domestic bliss—it wasn't jealousy that incensed her, it was the idea of his concealment. And then the thought: How much had Zachary loved his first wife?

His first wife. Christ.

That makes you his second. Suddenly.

She stepped inside the gallery, bracing herself. She saw people she knew, people she'd met at other gatherings and events, and it occurred to her that maybe the only difference between herself and her late mother was the fact that her mother had gone to the trouble of actually participating in functions, whereas she merely wrote about them—a perception that depressed her. She saw Marguerite in the midst of the throng, a plump little woman who wore her hair in the manner of a Spanish dancer, a sleek bun attached to the back of her head like some enormous black wart. Marguerite slid through the room and took Christy by the hand. Christy felt herself being yanked into a corner by the proprietor and thrust against the wall, a glass of something shoved into her fist.

"Drink, dear," Marguerite said. "It's the only way to survive these events, isn't it? Do you like my place? I had Horace of Manhattan do the decor. The beige walls and recessed lights are meant to be neutral, of course, so as not to overpower the canvases . . . ."

"Of course," Christy said, and sipped her martini, seeing the olive sink to the bottom like a squat slug.

"Do you like the paintings? We've got quite a selection of local talent here as well as the work of certain New York painters. If the gallery is going to have a theme it's eclecticism. I know my critics will say I'm playing it safe, of course, but it's always a difficult market around here—" The small woman's eyes were wandering the room, checking the credentials of guests, assessing and weighing the importance of each.

Christy finished her drink and went off in search of another; as she slipped across the room she tried to avoid eye contact with various people she knew—Professor Ogleby from Bristol College, who wrote, in incomprehensible terms, theater and art reviews for the *Chronicle*; Sandy

Lazenby, a designer of outrageous clothes that used a lot of peacock feathers; Andrew Stuckey, a fop whose family owned much of the land around Bristol. They were out in force this afternoon, she thought as she found the table of drinks and helped herself to a second martini. She stood, feeling like a wallflower, and surveyed the movement in the room: the first sip of the second drink buzzed to her head and the gallery seemed too bright to her all at once, the noise intolerably loud.

There was an open window in the back and she pushed her way toward it. Clusters of tobacco smoke hung around the recessed lights: choking, stifling. She greeted a few people casually and then she was at the rear of the room, alone in a space that seemed to have been designated as a kind of no-man's-land. Alone—and she liked it. She looked through the open window into a back alley filled with trashcans and at last, growing restless, she moved toward the row of canvases.

Eclectic was the right word for this collection tucked away at the back of the gallery. There were paintings that appeared to have been scrawled by schoolkids—primitive cats, flowers, landscapes. There were a couple of neo-Cubist affairs that even to Christy's untrained eye appeared hopelessly outmoded.

And then, tucked further back—as if it was meant to be concealed rather than displayed—something rather odd, menacing, startling in its own fashion, done in such a way that the painter might have savaged the canvas, unleashing a raw power that couldn't be contained by any kind of technique. Four hunched figures, amorphous bodies and terrified faces, each face haunted by a fear or tragedy that couldn't be defined, only described. She stepped back from this painting and as she did she became aware of somebody standing at her side. She knew, without turning, who the person was. And she also understood she'd been expecting him.

"Interesting painting," he said.

She glanced at him in silence. What she found herself remembering was the key he had so casually dropped on the table in The Dying Swan. Why had he turned up now? Hadn't her rejection been plain enough? She moved slightly away from him but remained close to the painting that had gripped her attention. He was wearing a dark blue linen suit, a white shirt open at the neck, and some kind of medallion hung against his chest. She could smell his cologne.

"Why are you here, Richie?" she said.

He continued to look at the painting. "Because I realize I made a very bad mistake the other day. And I wanted to apologize to you for it."

"How did you know to find me here?"

"By calling your office—"

"I see." She studied his face a moment, wondering about the sincerity of his apology. He looked glum, contrite, genuinely upset.

"I don't know why I gave you that key, Christy. I don't know what came over me—"

"Some might call it lust—"

He smiled. "Lust? I guess."

"Richie, you could easily find somebody else, you know that, don't you? It wouldn't be hard for you to prowl around this room and find a more accessible woman. Why me, for God's sake?"

He didn't answer her question, just shifted his weight around uncomfortably.

She looked at him. There was a soft light in his eyes and his fair hair shone. Then she turned her face back to the painting because it was the kind of work that, however crude, demanded your involvement.

As she looked at it, she said, "I want you to stop following me, Richie, because there's no future in it for you or me." And she thought about Zachary a moment, flirting with the idea of revenging herself for his lies and omissions by being more cooperative with Richie—but this notion was so small and vindictive that she shoved it aside.

"I think we can still be friends," he said.

"I don't really think so."

"Why not? Can't you forget my proposition?"

"Just like that? No, Richie. If we became friends, the same situation would crop up again—"

"It wouldn't," he said.

She shook her head. "Please, Richie."

"Try."

"Please—" And she studied the painting again, drawn into it by the eyes of the figures, wondering what kind of tragedy had caused them to look the way they did.

He was silent, leaning against the wall just behind her. After a time he said, "It's a pretty impressive painting."

She nodded. "But I wouldn't want it hanging in my house. It scares me."

"Why?"

"It's obvious. Look at those four figures, look how they're all twisted and hunched up because something is obviously scaring the hell out of them, something we can't quite see and can't understand."

"Christy," and he stretched his hand forward, lightly touching her arm.

Even though she wasn't looking, she still felt the eyes in the painting boring into her—as if they were searching her, overseeing her like four self-appointed guardians of her fate.

"We all make mistakes, Christy," he said. "We don't have to be punished for them the rest of our lives, do we?"

Now his expression had changed—he looked so much like a small lost dog that she thought she was going to laugh. Punished for the rest of our lives—wasn't that phrasing it just a little too strongly? He'd wanted her in his hotel room and she'd refused and now he was trying to reestablish things on another basis—that of uncomplicated platonic friendship. But was that possible? Could that be achieved? Christ, what am I thinking? Don't I have enough things on my mind with Zachary?

"I'll forget the key," she said. "I'll forget you ever gave it to me. And maybe we'll run into each other again around town. Like you're always saying, Richie, it's a small world."

There was a lean muscle working in his jaw, as if he was trying to hide either his irritation or his disappointment. For a moment she wanted to say: Richie, I'm sorry, I'm just not the kind of woman you need, I don't want to cheat on my husband. But why should she have to apologize for anything?

"Is that all you're going to say?" he asked.

"It's my best offer."

He said, "It's better than nothing, I guess."

And then he was gone, an abrupt departure, his slim figure moving through the crowd of people in the room.

She felt a certain relief. Perhaps he had gone from her life for good; perhaps he had gone to feed in more rewarding pastures. It was one complexity less, and one temptation she didn't need.

Leonora Huntington watched the handyman push a wheelbarrow across the lawn. When he was near the shed he stopped, put the wheelbarrow down, and then, because he thought no one was looking, scratched his balls vigorously.

She let the curtain fall from between her fingers. It always gave her some pleasure to observe people when they thought there wasn't anybody looking—at such times, you felt privy to certain things that were intensely personal. The secret observer: it was a source of power. She wandered across the living room and reached the hallway, where she stopped. Skyler, the butler, was going into the library. She called out to him and he paused, frozen in mid-stride. She enjoyed the obedience of servants (a luxury that Daniel Huntington could well afford to give her) and the look in their eyes when they were in her presence and awaiting her instructions.

"Have there been any calls for me, Skyler?" she asked.

He shook his head.

She nodded, watching him wait for a sign from her that he was free to go about his duties. She didn't give him one; he stood in a state of suspended animation, almost as if he defined his existence in terms of her whims and demands—which, she reflected, was more than a little true.

"Are you certain?" she asked.

"Certain, ma'am," he said, his voice devoid of any feeling.

"You can go," she said. Even then he hesitated, as if afraid she might rescind her command. "You can go," she said again, and this time the old man entered the library. She watched the door close and, clenching her hands, looked up the flight of stairs in front of her. No calls, she thought. She felt a slow burning anger at the back of her mind, but since she liked the idea of control, of never giving in to those emotions she considered base and unworthy of her, she pushed the sensation aside. No calls, she thought again: she realized how very unreliable he could be—and she had the sensation all at once of skating on fragile ice.

In the library Skyler was putting books back on the shelves in their correct order, like a man who is tyrannized by alphabetical sequences. He turned his white face toward her questioningly. She massaged a vein at the side of her head. Why hadn't he called? There was always that problem of other people keeping their word. Then again, perhaps there was a very good reason to explain his failure; perhaps he had nothing of any interest to report. And that would be unfortunate.

Then she raised a hand toward the books and slid a volume out, looking at the spine. "When I last checked the alphabet, Skyler, I was under the impression that B for Bellow came before C for Camus. However, you may be working from an entirely different and quite unknown alphabet—"

"I'm sorry, ma'am," he said.

She thrust the book at him, rubbing her fingertips together. And then she went to the window. She felt a quick rush of blood go to her head, as if some huge red band were cutting across her skull. She would choose to ignore it—but it was so damnably hard to push aside her rage whenever she thought about that wretched woman Zachary had married. What was her name?

Christy.

A stupid name altogether.

Leonora pressed her face against the glass and cursed Zachary for taking a wife without her permission—as if the last one hadn't been enough.

She turned and left the library. Inside the sitting room she found Daniel Huntington in his favorite armchair, a hardcover book open in his lap. He wasn't exactly asleep, although she could tell his eyelids were heavy. She sat on the arm of the chair so that her dress rose up her thigh, a sight she knew he found pleasing. He raised one hand and set it flat against her flesh.

"Do you love me?" he asked.

"Yes. You know I do."

He sighed quietly. She understood that she loved Daniel Huntington in her own fashion: the feeling did not have the same intensity as she'd experienced in the past toward, say, her brother, Zachary—this was altogether a different thing, as if variations of love could be measured on some emotional slide rule. If she had to choose a more appropriate word for her feelings about her husband she might have selected comfortable or pleasing rather than anything suggestive of passion. But she hadn't married him out of passion in any case. Now she ran her fingertips around the rim of his ear and he smiled.

"I love you," he said.

"I know," and she nodded. Fondness, she thought. On good days, I feel fond of him.

"You know what it does to me when you touch my ear like that, Leonora."

"I know only too well," she said. Not all loves could be the same—some burned with the ferocity of old ghosts on a funeral pyre. Some burned with the heat of the sun. And sometimes, unfortunately, there could be a problem in keeping that kind of intensity alive.

But she knew how to do it.

Even though there were times when it was very hard and extremely trying to hold things together, to exercise control over so many variables and to keep all the threads together, she knew she would manage.

She always had, of course.

She always had.

7

There was music playing in the hotel lounge, the kind of
music that is supposed to relax you with its soothing
anonymity, but he didn't feel very relaxed right then because
the stuff was grating inside his head, scraping along his
skull, irritating him. He stared across the room at his own
reflection in the mirror behind the bar; a big pink-tinted
mirror designed to make everybody look good. When he
saw his face he felt a moment of strangeness; he couldn't
relate to the image. He looked away, wishing the godawful
music would stop.

At times in the music he imagined he heard voices. Small,
whispering voices that sometimes called his name.

It is the unspoken law, Richie.

—people will not be allowed
to intrude

DO YOU UNDERSTAND?

People

are not going to step inside the circle no matter
what, Richie—

And these voices were disjointed, broken, like frag-

mented memories from a dead childhood. Like tiny, sad voices floating out across a half-forgotten fall afternoon when you could smell burning leaves and the air had winter in it—

But why does the past matter now?

Why?

There shouldn't be any turning back.

—you know what your duty is, don't you

you know what you have to do and that is the same as you did before

because people are not permitted to enter

the circle has to be closed tight—

He picked up his drink, a rum and Coca-Cola, sipping it slowly. He had to shake his mind free from the voices. But sometimes you just couldn't shake yourself free of everything that the past held prisoner, and you succumbed to old pains that were no less severe for their age.

He examined his fingernails and he thought: *What was it Christy said to you in that art gallery? All the time you thought you had her eating out of the palm of your hand and then she said:* See you around. Don't call me. Get lost. But he didn't want to think about her now; it was a failure, and failures embarrassed him.

He finished his drink and set the glass down.

Maybe he hadn't been convincing enough. Or maybe it had had something to do with that painting in the gallery. Those four figures looking down at you like that, it was bound to affect your mood.

He closed his eyes and he could see, as clearly as if it were in front of him, the painting on the wall. And for a moment it seemed to him that he was opening a door at the end of a long dark corridor and peering into a dim room, *barely making out the shape of a figure working in the bad light, hearing the sound of a chisel or something hard knocking and chipping against stone—and he could smell paint and dust and turpentine, even as the figure turned its face toward him. . . .*

He opened his eyes.

There was sweat in the palms of his hands; he picked up a paper napkin and ran it between his hands.

A dream, he thought. All that is a dream.

A dream of shapes. Of figures.

A woman stepped through the revolving doors, glass glinted. And for a moment he was shaken by a resemblance, a likeness he didn't need.

Something sharp. Sudden.

He got up from the table and followed the woman a little way along the lobby. She was slim and her hair long and she carried herself with grace. She stopped at the reception desk and he pretended to examine a newspaper while he watched her. You're wrong, Richie, wrong, wrong, wrong—there was no similarity. None at all.

He leaned against the wall. The woman moved away from the desk, smiling at him. For a moment he thought . . . Then he watched the doors swallow her and nudge her out toward the street.

He raced down the hallway and went outside, just in time to see her get inside a taxicab. A stranger. What made you see a likeness just then anyhow? You've forgotten, you've forgotten the way she looked and talked and smelled and walked, you can't bring back anything she ever said to you, can't remember the places you met her, nothing, a fat zero.

You can't remember anything at all, except her name. Anthea.

That—and a sense of an old hurt.

* * *

Zachary closed the manuscript folder and gazed across the room at Christy, who was sitting cross-legged on the sofa, a book open in front of her. She didn't seem to be reading; her eyes appeared to scan the printed pages without comprehension. She had been this way ever since she'd met him at the station—distant, silent, withdrawn. He wanted to get up and go across the room and say something to her but he didn't move.

Barriers. Obstacles.

But there was only one barrier really.

The past. Old history. Dead events. How did you contrive to get beyond them and teach yourself that only the present was worth inhabiting? A way—somewhere he'd have to find a way.

He sighed and she glanced at him, then went back to her book.

One barrier. He rose from his chair and wandered to the windows and looked out at the dark; the moon, half-formed, seemed flat and disinterested. He stuck his hands in his pockets and studied the night sky a moment. She's dead and there's no sense in bringing it up now, she can't come back, words wouldn't bring her back, she's dead and she owes nothing to the living—

He listened to a log slip in the fireplace; then there was the sound of Christy turning pages. He looked at his wife and he thought: It should be easy to say, I should not have this terrible difficulty in saying it—but the words lay inside him like something he couldn't digest. He walked slowly across the room, sat down on the rug beside the sofa and touched Christy's hand lightly. She looked up from her book, pushed hair from her face; and she gazed at him questioningly, her eyes serious.

101

She's waiting, he thought. She's waiting for me to tell her. He placed the palm of his hand against the side of her face and struggled to find the words—and then he was remembering his meeting that afternoon with Rucker, remembering the man Christy was said to have met in a bar; he'd spent the whole afternoon trying to suppress the image. A man, somebody Christy knew, somebody she'd never told him about—and a familiar fear went through his body.

Although he always fought the sudden upsurge of memory, struggled against the terrors of the past, now he yielded a moment and it was as if he were flicking through the dreadful pages of some dark photograph album.

Christy closed her book and looked at him. "I don't see how we can keep this up, do you?"

He shook his head.

"Zack, I didn't come into this marriage expecting to unearth your little secrets, did I? I came in anticipating honesty, at the very least—" She was lighting one of her rare cigarettes.

Honesty, he thought. Tell me about this man you met, Christy. Tell me about him. Maybe we could trade information, a kind of a barter system—you tell me about him and I'll tell you all about Anthea. He looked into her eyes: it wasn't anything that could be settled facetiously. The pages of the photograph album turned over inside his head, as if moved by ghostly fingers, and he saw Anthea standing on a street corner in the rain, her yellow plastic coat—so like the kind worn by little children—glistening, rain streaming through her hair and over her face, a rain that slithered across her skin in the manner of tears. And there was something else on the edge of the snapshot, a drugstore light and a man just coming into view, a man who walked briskly through the wet evening, a man to whom Anthea suddenly turned and embraced and kissed. Where were you right then, Zachary?

Sitting in a parked car and watching your wife across the street . . . trying to see her through the blurry rain that skittered down the windows.

Christy covered his hand with her fingers. "Look, I understand that there's something painful locked away here and I think I understand that it has to be something pretty damn bad for you not to tell me about it—but don't you see, it's got to come out into the open somehow, Zack? Don't you see that?"

He looked at his wife and wondered if there really was a resemblance between her and Anthea; maybe, maybe a slight thing, something he'd never been conscious of until Leonora had mentioned it. The idea terrified him: what if he had unconsciously tried to repeat the past? What if he was imprisoned inside a series of repetitions, doomed to be trapped there?

You don't want to think that way but you're conditioned because tragedies condition people—

"Zack, please," she said.

The smoke from her cigarette curled around his eyes and he blinked. "I want to talk about it," he said. "But the words don't come very easily, Christy."

"How did she die? Maybe you can start with that, Zack. How did Anthea die?"

He stood up suddenly and walked around the room, as if some small fire had been lit underneath him. How did she die? How had such a thing happened? He cracked his knuckles. There was a soft explosion of flame from the fireplace. Then Christy was coming across the room toward him.

"I want our marriage to be healthy," she said. "I don't want it to contain anything sick from the past."

He reached for her and held her tightly against his body. Something sick from the past, he thought. He shut his eyes, feeling her hair against his eyelids. The past. How to shape it, how to have it make sense, impose order on it?

"I love you, Zack. You know that, don't you?"

He could picture it now, he could see it quite clearly, the way the shower curtain had hung to one side as if tugged by a child, the way water had dripped from the faucet onto the enamel, the steady drumbeat of that sound, drip drip drip, the rustle of the night wind coming through the half-open bathroom window, the awkward cry of some bird in the darkness, he could see all this, but why couldn't he see Anthea?

The shower curtain. The bleak floral pattern.

The dripping water.

The window ledge with its row of toilet items—colognes and shampoos and razor blades.

Blades, he thought.

Blades . . .

He could hear Christy's voice coming to him from a faraway place.

"Zack. I want to understand. I want to know. Please . . ."

Razor blades.

The crooked shower curtain.

The dripping water, the water

and Anthea

Anthea lying in the tub, her arms stretched out at her sides, her feet turned outward

Anthea, white enamel, drip drip drip

He opened his eyes, looked at Christy.

"I found her in the bathroom," he said. "I was downstairs, I was reading . . . I don't remember really what I was doing, some of it won't come back even now—I don't know what made me go upstairs. Some strange urge—" He paused. It was only another few steps, a short distance. His eyes were moist and his nerves tight but he had to get this out, if only for Christy's sake. "I went upstairs to the bathroom and the door was halfway open and I remember calling out her name and there wasn't an answer, so I went inside the bathroom and I found her lying there.—"

Silence.

He took his hands away from Christy and moved toward the sofa, where he sat down and stared at the designs in the rug.

"She had taken a razor blade and she'd opened the veins in her arms. The tub was filled with her blood and there was this godawful sound of water dripping, I remember that . . ."

Christy put one hand to her mouth. "Why did she do that? Why?"

Zachary shook his head.

All the whys were lodged in the past.

Little mysteries of history.

But you have to get out of that place, Zachary. You have to tell yourself that this is a whole new life, you have to forge ahead on that basis, you do not need the whole damnable past to come leaping at you every time you draw a breath of air, you don't need the same chains around your heart every time you close your eyes or find yourself in a moment of solitude when the old thoughts come prowling around like wolves to a campfire.

But there are old debts, old allegiances, and they form bittersweet mazes around all your resolutions.

And there is Leonora, to whom you owe your life.

He gazed at his wife. "I'm not sure," he said. But you know, don't you, Zachary? You know the bottom line.

"Why would she kill herself?" Christy asked.

"Why does anybody?" he said.

Christy came and sat alongside him and took his hand, rubbing it gently. She looked at him thoughtfully, sympathetically, and then she said, in the tone people use when they change the subject, "How long had you been married?"

"Two years."

"What was she like?"

"Sometimes I can't remember."

Christy lit another cigarette. "Where did you live?"

Zachary got up from the sofa. He turned her question over in his mind: he had the feeling he was walking on somebody's grave. Where did you live? He looked across the room and imagined Anthea in the doorway, imagined he heard the soft sound of her feet on the rug, saw her drifting toward the window and looking out in that strange, slightly myopic way she used to have. This room, he thought. This room. Even if she was dead, she was still somewhere in this room, in this whole goddamn house. She'd never go away.

He looked at Christy helplessly.

And then he was gazing beyond her toward the doorway.

Christy turned, following the direction of his eyes.

"Here—" she whispered, and she swung her head around to look at him. "Here," she said again.

He moved to the sofa, reaching for Christy's hand.

"You lived here with Anthea, didn't you?"

There was a dryness at the back of his throat, a slight pulse beating at the side of his head. "Yes," he said.

"She killed herself in this house . . ."

"Yes."

"Upstairs in this house . . ."

Zachary sat back, shutting his eyes. Upstairs, upstairs in this house. *She killed herself upstairs.* . . .

Leonora watched her husband sleep in the armchair, his face tilted down toward his chest, his lips parted slightly. She walked around the sleeping figure for a moment, gazing at the skin of his bald scalp, at the network of fine veins running across his head. Daniel Huntington, peacefully asleep, dreamlessly so. She folded her arms beneath her breasts and went toward the French windows that led out to the garden. It was twilight; a solitary bird was whistling in a lazy fashion nearby. Leonora walked down the short flight of steps and paused by the flowerbeds. There was a faint fragrance in the air, a perfume that would soon be lost with the changing season.

Across the lawn from the direction of the shed she could hear the buzz of an electric saw and see the shadow of the handyman against the window. As she moved toward it, she tried to remember his name. Peter? Was that it? She always had a problem remembering the names of servants and employees.

When she reached the shed the young man killed the saw and wiped sweat from his forehead. The small room was filled with the smell of sawdust and shavings. There were stacks of planks piled up against the walls. She looked around the place, thinking how rooms associated with manual labor were always places of mystery to her. The strange tools hanging on the walls, like so many bizarre trophies, meant absolutely nothing to her: they might have been prehistoric finds for all she knew. Then it suddenly brought to mind her father's workshop, that narrow little room in which he hammered and sawed and chiseled. She could recall the smells of that place vividly now, she could see the way his lamp cast a yellowish light over surfaces, and she could remember the dead moths that adhered to the dirty bulb. My father, she thought: and she realized she hadn't considered the wretched man in years, that he'd somehow managed to slip mercifully out of her memory. Until now. Until this moment.

She pushed her chiffon scarf across her shoulder and smiled at the young man, who appeared somewhat embarrassed by her presence; with the dead power saw dangling in one hand, he was shifting his weight back and forth.

"You're working rather late," she said.

The young man grinned and nodded. "I like to finish what I begin," he said.

She studied him a moment. He was lean, narrow-waisted, his buttocks tight and trim in faded blue jeans. He had a mustache that reminded Leonora of a Mexican bandit, and he wore a sweatband across his forehead. On his upper right arm there was a tiny tattoo, a pale blue snake.

"I take it those are the bookshelves we discussed," she said.

"Right," he said. "I should be through by tomorrow, maybe the day after."

There was a silence; Leonora took the ends of her chiffon scarf and made a small knot of them. For a moment she was conscious of herself through his eyes—the Woman of the House, the Employer, the Boss. She thought she saw him glancing at her in a sideways manner, as if he was trying to look at her as a woman and not as the person who happened to pay his salary. What does he see? she wondered. A handsome woman of forty or so, someone who could pass for at least five years younger, well dressed, in control of things, never flustered. Somebody attractive, sexy. But he had to be conscious also of a barrier between them, a social divide.

"Why did you get yourself tattooed?" she asked. She lightly touched the misshapen snake.

"I don't know," he answered. "It seemed the thing to do at the time."

"At what time?" She rubbed his upper arm very softly, watching the guarded expression on his face.

"When I was in the navy," he said.

"The navy." She traced a line down his arm as far as his knuckles, seeing her darkly polished fingernails slide across his hand. "I didn't realize you had served your country, Peter."

The young man smiled uneasily. She knew what he was thinking, she could see it clearly on his face. She comes inside the shed and she starts to touch me and I don't know what she wants and whether I should respond . . . She licked her lips and tossed her hair back and then, smiling her best smile, her warmest one, she asked, "Don't you get lonely?"

"I read a lot. I like my work."

"Don't you get lonely for human companionship, Peter?"

"I don't seem to," he said.

"Tell me . . . what do you do for sex?"

"Sex?"

109

"You've heard of it, of course."

He seemed flustered. "I guess I . . . I don't think much about it."

She moved closer to him, letting her hip brush against his leg. He smells, she thought, he smells of sweat and wood and oil. He smells of this run-down little room, of a stale life, a life of soiled bedsheets and old *Playboy* magazines and things going rancid in the refrigerator. She shut her eyes: she didn't like to think about squalor. A world where people had dirty fingernails. Where they sweated. She wanted a world of clean forms, clean lines, a universe where things were always spotless.

"Do you like living here?" she asked. The smell of wood shavings filled her nostrils now: she thought it was making her very dizzy.

"Yeah, sure," Peter said.

She reached out her hand and let it dangle for a moment against his hip. His blue jeans were dusty, stained, and the material had begun to fray around the crotch and knees.

"I'm not sure . . ." he started to say.

"Not sure about what?"

"I mean, I kinda wonder why you're here, Mrs. Huntington."

"Here? In this shed?"

He nodded. She let her fingers drift away from his hip, let them touch the inside of his leg a moment before she moved away from him.

"Do you object to my presence in your little world, Peter?"

"Hey, I didn't mean anything like that—"

"Do you want me to go?"

The young man was uneasy; a single slick of sweat ran down beneath his headband.

"Or do you want me to stay awhile longer, Peter?"

"Mrs. Huntington," he said. "It's your property, I mean, if you want to hang out here, that's fine with me."

She stared at the saw in his hand, the sharp teeth that shone in the light. And she remembered quite suddenly that her father had had one just like that; it had hung on the wall above his workbench, and sometimes, when she was lying awake and trying to get to sleep, she'd hear the terrible rasping sound of the thing drone through the darkness, the sound bound up in her mind with the crying of small children, as if the two were inseparable.

Hush, she thought. Everything's fine, everything's going to be fine.

But there were the scents that always laced the darkness. Rust and urine and old clothing.

She raised one hand to her hair. Control, she thought. There is nothing quite so satisfying, so rewarding, as control. Control of yourself. And of others.

Like this young man at whom she was smiling again. Control of him.

"You were saying something about property," she said.

"Yeah," and he was looking at her curiously.

She moved a little closer to him. She placed her hand against his chest, and she could feel the quick heartbeat. The terror of the heartbeat. She snapped a shirt button open: in the dead center of his chest there was another tattoo, barely visible amidst all the curls of fair hair.

"Another souvenir of the navy, I imagine," she said.

He nodded: his mouth was open and she could see his small white teeth.

She lowered her head and kissed the center of his chest.

"Mrs. Huntington—"

111

She raised her face and smiled at him.

"Mrs. Huntington—"

"You find me attractive, don't you?"

"You're a very beautiful woman."

She closed her eyes and leaned against his shoulder and let her hand slide across his belly; she could hear him moan quietly, then she felt the rough palm of his hand go under her dress, the calloused fingertips slipping upward over her soft flesh.

She parted her legs only slightly as his hand moved further up her thigh and then she stepped away from him, her back pressed to the wall of the shed. He was staring at her in surprise.

"What's wrong? Did I do something wrong?" he asked.

She ran her fingers through her hair and looked at him without speaking; she could feel electricity course through her, a sense of some enormous power. Another life, she thought: for a moment there you could feel yourself holding another life in your hands, controlling the urges and desires of a human being separate from yourself, dictating their behavior to them, taking them to a place where whatever willpower they might possess had been weakened and subverted—

"What did I do?" the young man asked.

She shook her head and walked to the door of the shed; outside, twilight had gone and the darkness was complete. She stared at the trees, then at the lights of the house.

"What did I do? I don't understand. I mean, you come down here, you start to put out some pretty unmistakable signs, I'm only human, I react, then you just turn off the goddamn faucet. Does that give you your kicks, Mrs. Huntington?"

She still said nothing. She was no longer interested in the young man or his shed and planks of wood and tools. She was not interested in anything he had to say.

She began to cross the lawn.

From the doorway of the shed, the young man said, "There's a name for somebody like you, Mrs. Huntington. You know that?"

She neither knew nor cared. She reached the terrace of the house and glanced briefly in the direction of the statues, which in darkness had the appearance of ancient trees, stunted relics of another time. She thought: I should put spotlights on them. They would look fine if they were lit at night. She closed her eyes and rubbed the lids softly a moment.

Then, as she entered the house, she heard the grinding sound of an electric saw starting up.

Christy sat on the bed and gazed absently at the flickering TV in the corner of the room; electronic Valium, she thought, images and sounds to fill a vacuum. Little noises to deaden the whispers of her own thoughts. She'd heard Zachary moving around downstairs but he'd never come up to the bedroom, which was just as well—she didn't want to see his face right then. She didn't want to look at him or be in his presence; she didn't want to see the man who had brought her to a dead woman's house.

Try being rational, she thought.

He was married before, okay. The wife committed suicide, fine. And it just so happened that he brought his new wife to the same place where the former Mrs. McNair had killed herself, a whole story he hadn't gotten around to telling her—

113

Now, what was wrong with that, after all?

Jesus Christ. Everything was wrong.

This bedroom, for one thing. This bedroom contained ghosts. This would be the room where Zachary and his bride had made love. And when she thought about this she had the strange feeling that she had gate-crashed something very private; that she'd become a voyeur, or worse—a ghoul participating in a sinister, macabre ménage à trois. Did he ever think, as he made love to Christy, that it was Anthea who was clamped to his body? Did he ever let his mind wander that far?

And then there was the rest of this big house to consider. How could she live here, knowing that Anthea McNair had walked everywhere before her—other rooms, the lawns, the driveway? How could she live here without constantly being reminded that some poor woman had slit her wrists in the bathroom.

The bathroom, she thought.

Anthea was everywhere, she was pervasive, filling the house as surely as any living thing might. Her little touches, the impressions she had left, the relics of her energies—this whole goddamn house was filled with her.

A light burned at the far end of the hallway. Christy went to the top of the stairs and looked down. How many times had Anthea climbed these stairs? How many times might she have stood in this exact spot and looked down just like Christy was doing now?

Christy turned, went along the hallway, stopped.

The door of the bathroom was halfway open. The room beyond was in darkness.

How can you go into that room without being forced to face the horrible fact that Anthea McNair had taken a blade

114

and sliced her flesh open and let her life's blood seep out? Had lain in the bathtub and drifted off into the sleep of suicide?

Christy hesitated a moment. Then she pushed the door open and stepped into the room, fumbling for the light switch. And she wondered: Was it dark or light when you came this way for the last time, Anthea? Did you have to flick this same switch to find your way to your death?

The light was bright, the tiled walls gleaming, the mirror a disk of lit silver. Christy stared at her own reflection and wondered how many times Anthea had studied herself in this same glass—and then the house suddenly seemed a suffocating place to her, a huge tomb, a mausoleum in which she did not belong.

A place for the dead.

8

Daniel Huntington had not been able to sleep. He rose around dawn and walked across the bedroom to the landing, glancing back once at the shape of his sleeping wife. So still. So tranquil. And then he stared upward, conscious of the dark house rising above him as if it were an endless sequence of stories, shadows piled on other shadows. He pinched the bridge of his nose and thought: Leonora, I am too old to encounter new treacheries—and he remembered how she had gone across the lawn to the shed, how he had watched her from behind a tree and seen her touch the young man . . .

This was new, something he wasn't equipped to deal with.

He shut his eyes and wondered how long she might have been sneaking around behind his back and whether she had ever visited the young man in his cottage. Pictures crowded his mind—Leonora climbing into the young man's bed, her naked arms holding his body hard against her own. He tried to shove these images from his head; with each picture the pain was worse.

He moved to the foot of the stairs, looking upward; the darkness of the house seemed to seep through him. He realized he felt like a stranger in his own home, an outsider, someone without rights.

He had been excluded from things.

From his wife's world.

From her secrets.

From that damnable room of hers upstairs.

I should have been stronger, he thought.

I should have taken a stronger stand.

And he thought of that secret space in the upper part of the house. He could almost feel the vibrations come down to him through the dark.

What did she do up there anyhow? Why did she need that space?

In his mind the two things became connected—the young man and the room upstairs—as if they were twin aspects of the same sickness: Leonora's secrets.

He began to climb. Halfway up he paused and thought: She loves me, she told me she loves me. There had been times when he had never doubted her, never feared the loss of her love, times when he had experienced great joy. He could see her now, watch her undress and come into bed beside him; sometimes, when they had made love, they would simply lie together in a silence that was perhaps the most private thing in his whole world. The most intimate, the most peaceful. How could he lose such things?

He reached the landing and gazed at the next flight of stairs.

He was trembling very slightly. He stopped, thinking he had heard a sound from the lower part of the house. Perhaps Leonora had wakened and missed him. The thought filled him with dread. Was he afraid of her in some way? Afraid of his own wife? He shook his head and began to climb again.

A few more steps. That was all. Just a few more steps and then he'd stand outside the door of Leonora's private room. I should have done this before now, I should have insisted on entering the place, I should have asserted some kind of authority—

When he reached the landing he wondered if perhaps Leonora locked the place, if she had a key hidden away, but then it occurred to him that she might be arrogant enough to leave the room unlocked, thinking that neither he nor any of the servants would dare to violate her privacy.

He looked at the door.

He wiped the damp palms of his hands against the sides of his robe.

You shouldn't be doing this, he thought. No matter what betrayals Leonora has perpetrated, you shouldn't be thinking about entering her room in this way.

He approached the door, raised his hand to the grainy wood and hesitated, conscious of how hard he was shaking now.

He touched the handle.

He turned it.

The door opened a little way and he found himself staring into darkness.

A switch.

Fumbling for a switch.

Click—

The room was filled with a sudden harsh light.

This room. Her room.

118

It was the sound of her voice that jolted him, that made him swing around abruptly.

"What are you doing in here, Daniel?"

He felt his mouth hang open and his nerves scream.

"What are you doing in my room?"

He gazed at her face and realized he had never seen this expression before; her eyes were dark and her mouth tense and her hands, slightly upraised, had the appearance of claws.

"Nobody is allowed in this room," she said.

Something inside him gave way—strength, nerve; he wanted to apologize to her but his throat was dry and his tongue heavy and he couldn't find any words. And then she smiled and he saw that the smile was a cold thing. He thought: I am afraid of her.

He moved past her to the door, to the landing beyond.

Her precious room.

He shivered as he heard her come up behind him, her nightdress whispering against the floor.

That horrible white light.

He moved to the top of the stairs and looked down and he wondered—

What did I see in there?

What did I see in that room?

Enough.

Just enough.

At his back, Leonora slammed the door shut.

Christy had spent the better part of an hour chewing absently on the end of a pencil and looking out the window at the traffic in the street below. She had been turning over in her mind the prospect of going through the newspaper files, but what made her a little uneasy was the vague feeling she had of disturbing a grave, stirring up ashes of old history just to satisfy a curiosity that might be morbid. But it wasn't morbid at all, she thought. Didn't she have a right to learn something about the woman who had been Zachary's first wife and who had killed herself in the house where she, Christy, lived? What was morbid about that?

She gazed into the street; from the corner of her eye she was aware of Rossiter coming across the newsroom toward her. Today he was wearing yellow suspenders, which he kept flexing back and forth as he moved.

"You concern me, Christy," he said.

"Why is that?"

"You don't usually sit and chew pencils for hours. What's the matter? The social world gone off the boil? No fancy affairs to attend?"

She smiled at him.

"Trouble?" he asked.

She shrugged. "Maybe."

"Let me guess. Trouble is usually associated with two things. Money or marriage. In your case, I can't imagine it would be the former."

"Why?"

"Because, Christy, you are married to a man of substance. That's common knowledge. You're not in a position to worry about where the next lamb chop is coming from, are you? Ergo, I detect a marital problem. Am I right?"

"The marriage is fine," Christy said.

Rossiter scrutinized her.

"I don't like that look," she said.

"What look?"

"The judicious eye."

He reached out and touched her shoulder; he had a gentle, weary smile. "I don't mean to interfere."

"My ass," she said.

"Nicest ass on the whole newspaper, Christy." He paused. "Well, kid, my door's always open for you." Then he was gone across the room and back inside his glass-walled cubicle.

Christy went through the door that led to the morgue and the miracle of microfiche; all the back issues of the *Chronicle* had been stored and neatly filed on microfilm. She gazed at the rows of boxes, still uncertain about what she was going to do, feeling suddenly like a contestant on a game show who is undecided about whether to open the box or take the cash and just walk away. Hell, Zachary wasn't going to tell her anything, was he? So she would have to find out what she could about Anthea on her own.

Where to start? she wondered.

She went back three years. She put the file inside the microfiche machine, turned the thing on, and stared at the pages on the screen in front of her.

Obituaries. Columns of the dead.

She went through issue after issue, running her eyes over the names—and with each obit she felt more and more like a vulture. Sometimes there were small photographs of the dead, little snapshots which, in their grainy quality, seemed to have been taken by a photographer from the Other Side. A spirit cameraman.

So many dead.

So many withered flowers.

So many autopsies, caskets, prayers.

After an hour, she still hadn't come across the name of Anthea McNair.

She paused for a while because her head was beginning to hurt. Then she went back two more years. More obits, platitudes, graveside services. More photographs.

After two hours she had the feeling that this whole venture was fruitless; what if there hadn't been an obituary? What if Zachary hadn't wanted to publish one? She continued anyway, turning page after page and blinking at the words on the screen.

And then after two and a half hours she found what she was looking for.

She found Anthea.

There was a photograph.

Christy stared at it for a long time. The face that stared back at her was oval, framed by long dark hair. The eyes were big and somehow dreamy and the mouth suggested a slight petulance: it was like the mouth of a child accustomed to getting her own way. A pretty face. But she couldn't imagine Zachary married to this woman, couldn't imagine them together. My fault, she thought. A tiny jealousy all my own.

Services for Anthea McNair, 29, who died yesterday, will be held Friday at Bristol Methodist Church. She is survived by her husband, Zachary.

And that was it.

That was all.

Christy felt strangely cheated; it was as if there was another message locked inside this terse paragraph, something meaningful she was meant to search for between the lines.

She looked back at the paragraph.

Tell me, Anthea. Answer my riddle. Why did you kill yourself?

But it was a face designed for mystery, difficult to read.

Christy rubbed her eyes. Twenty-nine years old and dead.

She was about to turn off the microfiche machine when she noticed something at the bottom of the obituary, a parenthetical reference to another part of the newspaper: (See story, C 6).

Story?

What story?

Christy flicked the pages back until she came to page six of Section C.

The headline was brutal, tight.

LOCAL WOMAN'S SUICIDE

Police were called early yesterday morning to the home of publisher Zachary McNair, 333 Underwood Drive, Bristol, because of the apparent suicide of his wife, Anthea. Mr. McNair discovered his wife's body in the bathroom, where the deceased took her own life.

Police are treating the affair as a suicide, although Mrs. McNair left no note or letter. According to her husband, she had not been depressed lately, nor did she have a history of psychiatric illness.

Zachary McNair is a successful New York City publisher.

Christy read through this story a couple of times, searching for anything not immediately apparent. And then her eye was drawn to the photograph that accompanied the piece. It was one of those pictures which seems to depict a heightened kind of reality—white faces, white hands, ill-defined features, a photograph shot by a cameraman with no interest in the privacy of his subjects.

She could make out Zachary standing on the steps of the house and staring at two ambulance men who were carrying the wrapped body out. She could see a couple of policemen standing around in the manner of people who are uncertain of their exact function. In the background were a number of faces—the kinds of anonymous lookers who always seemed to accompany any form of tragedy.

Christy pressed her fingertips to her eyelids a moment, then stared at the picture again.

And it struck her that one of the background faces was familiar.

It was a poor shot, a bad likeness, and maybe she was mistaken anyhow—

Imagining something, something that went beyond any obvious connections, a relationship that defied her under-standing—

She stared again.

Maybe she was wrong—

It doesn't make sense.

But she knew she wasn't mistaken.

She knew the name of that figure tucked away in the background.

She knew.

She turned off the machine and gazed at the blank wall for a time.

What had he been doing there on the night of Anthea's suicide?

What had Richie been doing at the scene of her death?

* * *

When Zachary reached the restaurant he hesitated a moment before going inside. He could see Leonora seated at the far side of the room, surrounded by her usual complement of waiters. She attracted them because she had that mysterious quality called presence. Cigarette lighters flamed, empty glasses were always refilled, solicitous questions were asked of her. She was wearing a large black hat that shadowed her face. He crossed the large room, feeling the plush rug beneath his feet, then he sat down facing his sister. There were days, he thought, when Leonora's beauty could still your pulse, when you felt inferior just by looking at her.

Her hand slipped across the table and covered his. "Zachary, I'm so glad you could come."

"How could I refuse you, Leonora?"

She had a drink in front of her, a pink-colored thing that was probably Campari.

"I thought to myself that I shouldn't let one of my rare visits to Manhattan go past without calling my little brother for lunch," she said. "And the food here is rather fine. They do a pleasant duck in black cherry-and-ginger sauce."

"I hate duck," he said. He was thinking of Christy, thinking of the hurt look he'd seen on her face last night. It wasn't an expression he liked to see, the more so since he had been responsible for it.

Leonora smiled and her eyes took on a somewhat misted look, a softening of the light in the pupils. "When you say it that way I'm reminded of how you were when you were a small boy."

The past, he thought. She was as much anchored to the

past as he was. To the same shackles. He was filled with a longing for freedom.

"How is Christy?"

"She's fine."

"You must bring her over sometime."

Zachary was given a menu by a passing waiter and he flicked it open. Osso bucco. Shrimp Florentine. The dread duck. He didn't have an appetite. He closed the menu, ordered a gin and tonic.

"I'm still unhappy about your visit the other night," he said.

"Why? Did I do something wrong?"

"You mentioned Anthea—"

"Dear Zachary, how was I supposed to know that you kept secrets from your wife?"

He wanted to get up and leave, he wanted the gritty air of the streets, but he didn't move. You left only when it was apparent that Leonora had dismissed you. Never before. It had always been that way.

"I love this woman, Leonora."

"I have no doubts that you do. As you used to love Anthea."

"This is a little different."

"Indeed."

"I'm trying to live my own life."

"Zachary," and she stroked the back of his hand, as if they were lovers. "Some of us cannot lead our own lives. Some of us need dependencies. Some of us have bonds, bonds involving other people."

Bonds, he thought.

Always.

She smiled, an expression filled with warmth and love. It was the same smile that he remembered from childhood, and he suddenly wondered what right he had to feel, as he sometimes did of his sister, a resentment. She had always been able to take care of everything, all the aches and pains of childhood, all the bruises of a careless universe. She has always, he thought, taken care of me. But goddammit, it was past, it was a bad time, why couldn't they just put it away?

"We are bound together," she said. "We will always be bound together. It's never going to be different. Blood . . ." And she paused, her expression distant. "Blood is what protects us. We don't need strangers, Zachary. We don't need new blood."

New blood. Christy was new blood.

And Anthea before her.

Blood, he thought. It was always blood with Leonora, always that strange mystical bondage.

When I was a small boy, he thought, Leonora was the only kind of light.

But what was he supposed to do? Live forever in gratitude to her?

She was opening her purse now. She took out a photograph, a cheap black-and-white snapshot that was yellowy with age.

"I found this just the other day," she said. She handed it to him, but he didn't want to look at anything from that time. Nevertheless, he took it, turned it over slowly in his fingers and gazed at the picture, realizing he felt sick.

The picture was creased.

One crack ran diagonally across it.

He held it a moment, then let it flutter from his hand to the surface of the table. There was a pulse beating at the back of his neck. The picture lay against the stem of Leonora's glass.

"Did it upset you, my dear?"

A photograph. A simple picture.

He couldn't let it pain him like this.

Leonora picked up the picture and looked at it. "It's a good likeness of him, don't you think?"

Zachary nodded slowly. A good likeness.

He could sense an old terror turning inside him like a screw being tightened in the dead center of his chest.

"It brings back so many memories," she was saying.

Memories.

A man in a photograph.

Surrounded by pale sunshine in a black-and-white world.

That was it.

That was all.

This pounding. This awful hammering.

"Zachary, you're pale. Are you unwell?"

He realized he was trying to get up from the table but that his limbs wouldn't work. And he found himself gazing at the wretched photograph again.

Just a man. Just a person you don't have to remember now.

He struggled finally to his feet.

"Where are you going, my dear?" Leonora asked.

He moved across the room and went out into the street until he felt the wind push against him.

When he came to a corner he paused.

The wind was making it hard to breathe.

That photograph—

It had been her way of reminding him, as if he needed it, of something he was not meant to forget. Not ever.

He crossed the street, vaguely aware of the fact that he had an appointment back at his office, even though he couldn't remember when or with whom. Everything seemed curiously blurred to him except for the picture she had somehow found.

He had to get it out of his mind.

He had to.

He didn't need a photograph to remind him of the past.

He didn't want to be reminded of anything from that time.

Especially his own father.

Especially that.

He watched her leave the office of the Chronicle *and then she was going across the parking lot to her Jaguar. He hurried, catching her just as she was opening the door of her car. Her expression didn't change when she saw him— she was neither pleased nor displeased, there was no look of surprise, no impatience, nothing.*

"I'm sorry," he said.

"For what?" she asked, and her voice was flat.

"For leaving the gallery like that. I guess I felt disappointed."

"Why are you always apologizing, Richie?" she asked. "Your conscience troubling you?"

"My conscience?" He laughed briefly. "I don't think so." He paused a moment. "I just wanted to say I was sorry about the way I behaved, that was all. I guess I wanted more out of a relationship with you than you were prepared

*to give. Your husband's a very lucky man." Zachary, he
thought. Lucky Zachary. "Will you have a drink with me?"*

She shook her head. "I don't think so, Richie."

"Please?"

"No."

"I'd still like to be friends—"

*"Friends don't sneak around behind your back. Friends
don't play games, Richie."*

"Games? What games?"

"I don't have to tell you, do I?"

*"I'm sorry, but you're losing me, I wasn't playing any
games—"*

*She put her hands in the pockets of her suede jacket and
she looked suddenly quite beautiful, the late-afternoon sun
touching her hair, and her eyes bright. "Who are you,
Richie?"*

*What kind of question was that? he wondered. "You
know who I am," he said.*

"The hell I do."

*He stared across the parking lot at a garbage truck
roaring. What was wrong with her? Why was she taking this
approach with him? He felt a moment of uneasiness.*

*"Tell me why you were at my husband's house the night
Anthea died. Tell me that, Richie. Give me a good
convincing explanation for that coincidence, if you think
you can!"*

"Who is Anthea?" he asked, and his throat was dry.

"Why were you there that night?"

"You're wrong, you're very wrong, Christy—"

"I don't think so. You must remember Anthea."

The garbage truck was picking up trashcans with its

grinding hydraulic lift. It seemed to him that the noise originated inside his own head.

"Christy, please. You're talking in puzzles—"

"Tell me all about puzzles," she said.

Anthea, he thought. He reached out and caught the sleeve of Christy's jacket. He realized he wanted this woman, he wanted her quite badly right now. But why was she talking about Anthea?

There hadn't ever been an Anthea. There hadn't ever been a sad-faced young woman who lay in a bathtub with her own blood draining out of her.

There hadn't ever been the love letters and the clandestine meetings and the old passions.

He raised his hands, placing the palms flat against the sides of Christy's face. There was defiance and anger in her eyes now and she stared back at him as if she meant never to blink again in all her life.

He hesitated a second before lowering his hands to his sides.

The desire he had felt changed, withered inside him, turned to a different feeling altogether. There was anger, the color of wine, rising in his mind.

I want to hurt her, he thought.

He watched her open the door of her car and get inside, he heard the engine turn over and then she was driving out of the parking lot, not looking back, not looking back at him once.

He stood for a long time after she'd gone.

He stood watching the garbage truck crunch trash, fish bones and old boxes and discarded papers. Great plastic bags stuffed with refuse.

They had carried Anthea out of the house that night

*inside a plastic bag, carried her down the stairs and out
into the pale white ambulance; then they'd closed the doors.
And he remembered her face as she'd been hauled past him,
drained and bleached and dead.*

It might have been the memory of a dream.

Someone else's.

9

A house changes.

It alters.

It becomes something other than your house.

Something unfamiliar.

She parked the car and stared at the facade of the place and what she saw was that terrible photograph taken on the night Anthea died, she saw the nameless faces of the officials standing around, Zachary, she saw Richie hooded in shadows.

She rubbed her eyes and stepped out of the car. She didn't want to go inside the house. She couldn't face it.

Haunted, she thought—and even as she stood there looking up she imagined somebody was watching her from an upstairs window. Come on, Christy, you're being perfectly silly. You know just how silly you're being, don't you?

She rattled her keys in the palm of her hand.

Then she went up the steps, stuck the key in the lock, opened the door.

Inside the kitchen she gazed at the dishes in the sink from

that morning's breakfast, the skillet on the stove—and she could imagine Anthea working in this room, standing at the stove, stirring something, running water into the sink, pressing the buttons on the dishwasher, she could feel Anthea's presence in this large room as surely as if she were here in person.

Christy sat down at the table.

She felt very weary and her eyes still ached from peering through the microfiche machine. She got up, found a couple of aspirin, swallowed them with a little water.

This house. This unwieldy house.

She could almost feel it press down on her.

She went inside the study and stared at Zachary's desk.

There was a pile of papers, typescripts flowing out from folders, a bunch of correspondence, bills. She sat down behind the desk and let her hands wander over all the papers. And she thought: He must have cleaned out the house after Anthea's death, he must have gone from top to bottom of this large house, getting rid of all the traces of the dead woman, her clothing, her personal papers, everything. A kind of deathly spring cleaning. A funereal task.

She tried to imagine him picking up a blouse here, a dress there, stuffing all her cosmetic items into a bag or a suitcase—how difficult it had to be to obliterate the signs of an existence, and then to pretend that the woman had never lived at all. She wondered what that had done to Zachary's mind, that kind of retreat. She felt suddenly sorry for him.

The signs of an existence wiped out.

Tubes of used lipstick. A toothbrush. Combs.

But how could all the relics of somebody's life be erased entirely? How could somebody just pass through and leave no traces the way Anthea appeared to have done—an obituary, a brief story and nothing else? Christy walked around the room, trying to rid herself of the persistent sensation that there was another person in this house.

She moved out into the hallway and stood at the foot of the stairs. And again she wondered why Richie, of all people, had been here that night. If there was an association, she couldn't see it; if there was a connection, she couldn't make it.

She went up the stairs and inside the bedroom and looked at the unmade bed. Was it the very same bed Anthea had slept in or had Zachary had the delicacy to change it? A life doesn't disappear without leaving some sign in its passing, some kind of fragmented map.

But what? Exactly what?

In the reflection of the bedroom mirror she appeared ragged, washed-out, limp. Then she stepped out into the hallway. Inside the bathroom she avoided the sight of the tub and opened the medicine cabinet. She looked at the shelves: what kind of things had Anthea stored here? On the last day of her life had she opened this cabinet and taken out the fatal razor blade? Christy shivered. Traces. Tiny radar soundings left behind by a life—surely there had to be something of Anthea's in this big house?

She went back along the hallway and paused beneath the trapdoor that led to the attic, realizing that she'd never gone up there. There hadn't been any need. Nor was there any now, except— She tried to push the prospect aside. Be reasonable. You don't have to go poking around the dust of an old attic.

Christ, would Zachary have stored Anthea's stuff up there?

She let her hands hang limply at her sides and thought:

Don't go up there, don't let yourself get drawn upward into that room. You climb up there and it's an admission of something—like saying to yourself: Girl, you're growing pretty obsessed with a dead woman, which isn't exactly a healthy thing to admit. She went back inside the bedroom, fetched a chair and positioned it just beneath the attic door.

You still have time to put the chair back and behave like a reasonable person.

Plenty of time.

She clambered up on the chair and, stretching, drew back the bolt of the door, sliding the whole thing aside and staring up into the grim dark of the space overhead, assailed by a smell of dust and dampness and shapeless things concealed from sunlight too long.

There's still time to go back, Christy.

She hauled herself upward, muscles straining.

And then she was inside the attic room, surrounded by darkness, blinded, feeling the silky entrails of cobwebs float against her face like fragile living tissue.

A place like this—it was like discovering your house had another side to it, a split personality. Dark rooms you never visited, spaces you didn't go to.

She raised her hand and found a drawstring for the light. When she pulled it the attic was filled with a feeble yellow glow from the bulb that hung beneath a length of rotted cord. She blinked.

The room was larger than she'd imagined, filled with all kinds of junk, as if generations of residents had simply hauled all their refuse up here and abandoned it. Stacks of old newspapers, piles of insulating material, cardboard boxes with layers of thick dust. She moved toward the center of the attic and surveyed the chaos. Old broken furniture, an ancient oval mirror, the legs of tables—she wondered how much of this stuff had belonged to Zachary, if any of it ever had; somehow she couldn't see him laboring in the dust of this place.

She stepped over a pile of newspapers. Yellow, brittle and, as she saw from glancing at them, more than thirty years old, left here presumably by a resident other than Zachary or Anthea. There were stacks of mildewed books placed against one wall. She flipped a couple of them open—they contained no names, no marks of ownership. Mainly they were kids' books. For a moment she imagined that they might have belonged at one time to Zachary, but that wouldn't make any sense—why would he store his childhood library up here? And then she realized she didn't know how long he had occupied this particular house, whether he'd bought it when he married Anthea or even earlier than that.

Blank spaces.

Things she didn't know.

Then there were old clothes, most of them in the style of the 1950s, maybe even the late forties. Spiders scurried across the folds of the material.

She picked her way back across the room, stepping around things that lay in her path.

And then she found the window.

It surprised her—she hadn't known there was a window in this attic. It was small and round and very dirty. She took a sheet of newspaper and cleaned the pane of glass enough to look through. She stared out for a while. There was a perfect, uncluttered view of the driveway and the gates beyond. She gazed at the trees, at the fading sunlight of the fall afternoon and she thought: You could see anybody coming toward the house from this window. You could stand here and keep watch for anybody arriving, which was something you could not do from any other part of the house—because of the trees and because of the bend in the driveway.

She realized she didn't want to spend any more time up here. But then her attention was drawn to something else tucked away in a corner.

There was a pile of old canvases stacked against the wall.

Old canvases, hardened paintbrushes, squeezed-out tubes of oil paints.

Somewhere in the history of this house there had been an artist.

The canvases had been arranged facing the wall. She reached for the first one and turned it around to look at it.

Surprised, she stepped backward, blood rushing to her head.

She had seen this canvas before. Or one very similar to it.

In the Gallery Marguerite on the day of its opening.

Four figures, four figures frozen as if in terror and confusion, shapeless things that seemed only marginally human. She picked her way through the other paintings. Five in all, and each one almost the same as the last, as if the artist had single-mindedly pursued an obsession—that of getting these four figures absolutely right. Over and over and over, the same faces, the same emotion, the same vitality. She bent down and looked for a signature.

It was small, tucked away in the lower-right-hand corner of each canvas.

SM.

Just SM and no date.

She gazed at the top canvas once more and what she felt

this time was a deep impression of madness, of an inner struggle that could be resolved only in insanity; the picture plunged her into a world she didn't understand, a place of violent dreams, crazy urges, shadows so intricate you couldn't find your way through them and back into daylight.

Why were those canvases here?

Because the painter had once lived in this house, obviously.

SM had once lived in this house. The mysterious SM. But—

Why did she have trouble accepting all this?

There were outrageous coincidences here that disturbed her. The coincidence of seeing the painting in the gallery in the company of Richie. The coincidence of Richie's face in the newspaper picture. But coincidences were locked rooms to which you couldn't find the key.

And what the hell was the key here?

She walked toward the drawstring for the light bulb and was about to reach up for it when she stopped—

There was a large trunk stuck behind a heap of cardboard boxes, its rounded lid illuminated by the faint glow of the electricity.

Embossed on the lid, in gilt letters, was the name ANTHEA MCNAIR.

For a moment Christy hesitated. Why would she want to look inside a dead woman's trunk? Then she went toward it and laid her hands against the lid, feeling the dust. The hinges of the thing creaked as she opened it slowly and some enormous insect scuttled across the back of her hand. She recoiled briefly and then she had the lid open and was looking inside, trying to imagine Zachary packing this thing and hauling it all the way up here.

Clothes. Simple cotton shirts, dresses, little boxes that contained modest jewelry, plain bracelets and earrings and necklaces. Halfway through the pile, Christy stopped; she had the feeling that she was plundering a crypt, sifting the items of the dead for anything of value—but what do you expect to find here? What of value? Blue jeans, camisoles, a couple of unattractive evening dresses, shoes and sneakers. The essence of a person reduced to a stack of discarded clothing. Sad, she thought. And then she was at the bottom of the trunk.

Where she found a manila folder.

She slipped it out, opened it directly beneath the light bulb.

There were papers inside. A couple of sheets of thin unlined paper on which somebody, presumably Anthea, had scribbled words. The handwriting was shaky, spidery, consisting of uneven loops and hastily joined letters, as if the writer had been working in a fury. And most of it was illegible.

Christy narrowed her eyes.

These were drafts of love letters. Or that was what they appeared to be.

But it was so hard to make anything out of the scrawls that coursed across the paper.

> dear . . . when I . . . unhappy . . .
> that last time . . . things going so
> wrong . . . killing me . . .
> sometimes it just seems an illusion
> . . . but I don't see how I can get out
> of this alive . . .

140

Christy stopped reading. Love letter, suicide note—which? What was it that was killing Anthea? And who was the "dear" referred to in the letter?

Zachary?

It had to be.

Who else?

Christy turned the sheets over. There was more of the same.

> what I know now . . . sad . . .
> scared . . . I can only see . . .
> no exit . . .

What bleakness, Christy thought.

Why had Anthea been so utterly miserable?

Could it have been on account of Zachary, something he had done?

She closed the folder and what she wished now was that she hadn't found the thing: she was depressed. *I can only see no exit*. Jesus Christ, Christy thought, if these words were any indication of Anthea's state of mind, it was no wonder that she had sliced her own wrists open. But what was it that had brought her to this point?

She opened the folder again, flicking through the sheets.

On the last sheet, among the scrawls and scribbles and the words that had been inked out, she found the sentence:

> *the real . . . comes from L*

The real what? Christy wondered—and she went as close to the light bulb as she could to read the scratched-out word. The real something or other comes from L—it was like a cryptic clue in a difficult crossword puzzle.

It looked like "force" but it could easily have been something different.

Christy was only sure that it began with an F.

It could just as easily have been "fear."

And who was L?

Only Leonora, she thought.

She shut the folder and put it back in the trunk where she'd found it. Then she rearranged the clothing and pushed the lid down. Leonora—what had Anthea been trying to say about Leonora?

Christy had no idea what kind of relationship existed between Leonora and Anthea. And she had the feeling that whatever was trapped in the past was like a voice silenced a long time ago. The words were no more than old whispers she couldn't hear.

Old, dead whispers.

She had to get out of here immediately, her heart suddenly trapped in her chest.

Racing downstairs to the kitchen, she poured herself a small shot of Scotch and turned her mind back to the coincidence of the paintings. She picked up the telephone and dialed the number of the gallery. When she got through she heard Marguerite's voice, hushed and somehow secretive, as if she were talking in a public library.

"Christy, my dear, I meant to thank you for the piece you wrote about my gallery—"

"I'm happy you liked it." She picked up a pencil and began to tap it on the scratchpad next to the phone. "Can I get some information out of you about one of your artists?"

"I don't see why not, Christy."

"I saw a certain painting in your gallery. I'm not sure it had a title. It showed four figures—"

"I know the one you mean. A rather creepy thing."

"Right. I thought I might interview the artist."

"I wish I could help you, but I'm in the dark myself about the painter."

"What do you mean?"

"Well, about five weeks ago a little man came into the gallery with a portfolio of work. He told me he was representing the artist—whom we know only as SM—so we took one painting on consignment. And that's about it, Christy."

"You must have an address for this person."

"Sure. I'll look it up for you." A long silence. "Here we are. The man's name is Leon Coldwind and he's a lawyer in Manhattan—64 East Thirty-seventh Street."

Christy wrote this down. Then she turned her mind back to Anthea's scribblings.

The real force is Leonora.

The real fear is Leonora.

The real what?

She shut her eyes. Her own home was slowly becoming overcrowded with ghosts, noisy with the rattling of specters.

Leonora sipped her tea, then set the cup down in the saucer and looked across the room at her husband, who was sitting with his face turned away from her, the light from the window falling across his skin in such a way that he looked old, cheeks hollowed out, eyes ringed by wrinkles. She remembered how, after she had found him in her room, he had come to bed and begged for her forgiveness, going down ridiculously on one knee and imploring her. She rose and went closer to his chair.

He turned his eyes slowly toward her. And she saw something in his expression that reminded her of how Zachary had looked when she'd shown him that old photograph of their father. A touch of fear, a vague awe, perhaps.

"What are you thinking about?" she asked.

"I love you, Leonora."

"I know," and she let her hand fall on the back of his a moment, touching the upraised veins.

"What happened last night won't happen again," he said. "I promise you that. Everyone needs their privacy."

She nodded. Of course it would never happen again; for one thing, she intended to install a lock, which is what she should have done before. She smiled sweetly at Daniel. "What did you think of my room?"

He didn't say anything; a clouded expression crossed his face, as if he were guarding himself against the possibility of saying something he might regret. Touching the side of his face, Leonora turned away to the window. She could see Peter go across the lawn, pushing a wheelbarrow filled with crisp dead leaves. And suddenly she remembered it had been on a fall day such as this when they had put Anthea's body in the ground. Poor, silly Anthea, her head filled with dreams. She thought she knew so much, didn't she? She thought she had reached an understanding of things, but she had never known the real nature of blood ties. Dear, dead Anthea.

She could hear Daniel get up from his chair and come across the room toward her. On the day she had married this man there had been, if not love, then a certain tolerance of him; there had been the realization of what he could provide for her as well as his kindness toward her. She had felt secure enough to marry because she'd thought that the past was bolted down, controlled, everything in its place and locked away—but then Zachary, in an impetuous act of the heart, had married Anthea.

Once was bad.

This second time was worse.

Your duty, she told herself, is to safeguard matters. Your duty is that of keeping love intact, those ties of blood a sacrosanct thing. That is your duty—and the thought of Christy went across her mind now. Christy. She was suddenly impatient. Why hadn't she received the telephone call she had been waiting for? Why hadn't he called her?—and she tried to remember the name of the hotel where he was staying but momentarily it eluded her.

Daniel Huntington said, "I saw you, Leonora."

"Saw me?"

"In the shed."

"The shed, dear?"

"With the young man—"

She swung around and faced him. There was a desperate expression of hurt in his eyes. She couldn't stand that look, that awful vulnerability inscribed on his features. The shed, she thought. He had been spying. Creeping around, spying. But she wasn't going to accuse him of that because that would have been a strategic mistake. She raised one finger and ran it lightly along his cheek.

"I had been meaning to talk with you about that young man," she said.

"Yes?"

"His approaches to me have been offensive, Danny. I imagined he would simply stop. However . . ." and here she paused, searching his eyes, seeing how he was waiting

145

hopefully for any straw to clutch. "But since they haven't, I rather think it's time you dismissed him."

"Is that what you want?"

"Yes. You didn't imagine we were having some kind of relationship, did you?"

"I wasn't sure—"

"You're being very silly. He asked me to look at some shelves he was building and I'm afraid he got me there under false pretenses. Poor Danny. You must have imagined all kinds of things, didn't you?"

"Yes." He held her tightly against him. "I love you, Leonora."

"I know you do."

"I wouldn't know what to do without you."

"Will you dismiss the young man?"

"Immediately."

He was smiling now, as if all his doubts had been blown away. The sun was shining again in his little world. She thought* How easy it is. How very simple it is when love is one of your weapons.

She held his hand between her own and brushed the skin with her lips, as if this brief kiss were a way of sealing the commitment he had just made. She wouldn't be sorry to see the young man go. Anything that complicated her life was intolerable.

Like Christy, she thought.

But Christy's time was coming.

Christy's time was fast approaching.

"I'm happy we were able to clear up that little misunderstanding, Danny. I've been faithful to you all the time we've been married. I'm just surprised you would think otherwise, that's all."

"I went a little crazy imagining you with somebody else—"

"You have to learn to trust me, dear."

"Yes," and now he was smiling, humming under his breath, alive again.

"I have some things to attend to," she said. "Certain business matters."

He didn't ask what: everything was right in his universe again and his wife was faithful and he was loved. She kissed him softly on his forehead and then she left the room. Inside the library she shut the door and went to the desk, where she picked up the telephone. She tried to remember the name of the hotel. It was that big brownstone building in downtown Bristol. What was it called?

When it came back to her she asked Information for the number and dialed it. The phone rang for such a long time that she thought he had to be out somewhere—but then she heard his voice, a weary sound, as if he'd just wakened.

"I have been waiting for you to call," she said.

There was a long silence.

"Well?" she said.

And when she heard him sigh she realized that he'd achieved nothing. That he'd accomplished absolutely nothing.

She tapped her fingers on the desk. She was conscious of a threat as if it were a shadow lengthening inside her mind. *Christy.*

Why had Zachary taken a second wife? Why had he so disturbed the delicate balance of things?

She said, "This marriage has to be broken. One way or another, it has to be broken. Do you understand that?"

"Yes"—and his voice was a whisper.

"You remember Anthea . . ."

"Yes . . ."

"Then you know what you have to do, don't you?"

Another silence.

"You know what you have to do, don't you, Richard?"

And she put the receiver down with a certain finality. Then she walked to the window where she could see Daniel Huntington go across the lawn in the direction of the shed.

He stopped.

He could see the young man make a bonfire from dead leaves. Flames, blue and yellow and red, rose upward into the afternoon sky and then died out, leaving the pile smoldering darkly.

You want to believe Leonora, he thought.

More than anything else.

He felt the late sun beat against his face and a faint wind shift through the trees.

The lying bitch—

Those terrible, transparent lies—

He stared at the young man, who was naked from the waist up, as he tried to get the pyre of leaves going again.

Her room, he thought.

He rubbed his hands together and he thought: I should never have gone there. Never.

You step across a threshold and you don't know what you're going to see.

You can't imagine—

But under chill white lights it comes to you.

Fragments of a puzzle.

He started forward, then he stopped again, watching Peter.

It isn't your fault I have to dismiss you, Peter, he thought.

It's Leonora's fault. My wife. The wife I love. The wife who seems so often like two different people—the one considerate, loving in bed, kind and patient with a man who is older than her by too many years; the other a furtive liar who manipulates me, controls me, holds dominion over my emotions . . .

He sensed all around him the swirl of chaos, hearing the fissures and fault lines that were cracking open along the surface of his marriage—and realizing, with pain, that the woman he loved was someone he didn't really know and didn't even begin to understand.

He stared at Peter.

Then some faint intuition made him turn and glance at the house.

From upstairs, in the window of her precious room, Leonora was watching him.

10

The darkness was filled with the noise of crickets, a faintly panicked sound that came out of the trees. Zachary stood at the open kitchen window and looked at Christy, who was seated at the table, turning the pages of a newspaper. The sound of the sheets being flicked underscored her silence; she was burying herself in the newspaper because she didn't really want to talk about what was on her mind. He suddenly wanted to cross the kitchen and yank the newspaper away from her—instead, he sat down and faced her.

"How was your day?" he asked. My love, he thought. I have brought you pain.

"I went to the office. I did some work."

There was something in her voice, a faint quiver. He wondered if she was lying to him, and his mind hovered around the idea of the man, the idea that perhaps she had met her mysterious man somewhere. No, not now, he thought. You don't need these precipices, these valleys.

He got up, kissed the back of her neck, then wandered around the kitchen in a restless fashion. Her man. Her stranger. The simple thought of this was like something tight, as lethal as nylon rope, being drawn round his neck. He leaned against the sink, arms folded, and he studied his wife—aloof, withdrawn, as if she had stepped into a dimension to which he was denied access.

"Tell me," he said.

"Tell you what?"

"What's on your mind."

She raised her face from the newspaper and looked at him with a serious expression. "There's something I'd like to know, Zachary."

"What?"

"Something about this house."

The house. She hadn't absorbed the fact that Anthea died here. . . . Could she ever? He was tense and the tension created a knot in the center of his chest.

"Do you know anything about the people who used to live here?"

"No."

"Before you. Before you and Anthea, I mean."

What was she driving at? Where was she trying to go? He couldn't answer her.

"I mean, who did you buy the house from?"

"Some realtor. I can't remember."

"You must remember—"

"I don't, Christy."

"You don't remember the name of the family you bought this place from? You don't remember the name of the realtor?"

"No—" He licked his lips, which had become dry, dry as the tongue that seemed leaden in his mouth now. "Why these questions?"

"It doesn't matter." She lit a cigarette; she'd been

smoking more lately, he noticed. He slumped back in the chair at the table. He was weary all at once, fatigue going through him like a slow blade.

Tilting back his face, he imagined he could hear voices echoing in other rooms of this house, he could hear the slamming of doors, the sound of somebody whistling, the pain of a child crying. He rubbed the side of his head.

"Christy," he said. "I love you. I love you very much. I'm sorry I didn't tell you about Anthea before and I understand how it must bother you to be in this house." Christ, he was trying, he was really trying.

"I don't feel like I belong here," she said. "It's like you go inside a room that's always been familiar, except one day it's different and you're not sure how."

He should have gone from here a long, long time ago. But Leonora had wanted him to stay, that had been her wish, and he had complied with it as he always complied with his sister. All those acquiescences now seemed to him a summary of his failure. What was important in his life, for God's sake? Leonora's wishes or his marriage to Christy?

The bind, he thought.

Trapped.

Christy moved slightly away from him, picking up a napkin and raising it to her lips, and then she was crying quietly—but she pushed his hand away when he tried to comfort her.

"I can't help my curiosity, can I?" she said. "It comes with my profession. I just can't help snooping around attics and seeing coincidences every place I look."

Attics, he thought.

Snooping around attics.

"You went up there?" And he was thinking about

Anthea's trunk, her clothes, her scribbled papers which appeared to have been written in a private hieroglyphic. Suddenly the memory of the dead woman screamed at him, a long cry rising from a dark place.

"For the fun of it, Zachary. For the sheer hell of it."

"Why?"

"I was curious about Anthea—"

"And you found her trunk."

"I found her trunk, right. I found her sad little manila folder too."

Zachary shut his eyes a moment. The attic. He hadn't been up there in a long time. Attics always seemed to him that part of a house which contained historical detritus, things rejected and forgotten.

"And I found some old canvases," she said.

"Canvases?" If he listened very carefully, he could hear soft footsteps hurrying behind him, catching up with him.

"Strange paintings. Kind of haunting."

"Somebody must have left them there"—and there was a weird echo inside his head.

"Obviously," she said. "But who?"

"Is it important?"

She was silent for a time, not looking at him. "I looked up Anthea's obituary today, Zachary."

Why did this stun him? He should have anticipated it.

"She was very pretty. Pretty and sorrowful."

"Why did you do that? Why did you do such a thing? Ever since you learned about her you've developed this morbid interest in her and you do nothing but pry into the past. I don't know what the hell you expect to find—"

"Answers."

"Answers to what! I don't even know the questions you've got in mind—"

153

She said, "I read the story, I saw the photograph——"

"Jesus, are you really going out of your way to be cruel, Christy? Are you trying to hurt me by dredging up all this stuff? You're doing a damn fine job of it."

"Why would I hurt you? I love you."

"Then you'll drop this obsession—it causes me great pain, Christy, don't you see that?"

He had to get out of this room, out of this house, go outside and breathe the deep dark clean air. He moved into the hallway and he could hear her hurrying after him.

"Zachary——"

He reached the front door, hauled it open, stared out into the darkness. He could see the faint outlines of trees in the distance and beyond that the faraway lights of cars. And then Christy was touching him, her hand over his shoulder.

"What is it, Zachary? What are you so afraid of?"

He leaned against the doorjamb. Afraid, yes, yes, yes, so much so that he could smell it rising from his own flesh. Afraid of losing this woman, afraid of the great tentacles of the past reaching out to him, scared of his own impotence, his lack of real courage.

He went down the steps and across the lawn. Then he was going down the slope where the trees were thickest, the shrubbery wild. Thorns tore at his clothing and ripped the flesh of his hands. He came to a clearing, where he sat down.

He recognized this place.

He knew this place only too well.

This was where the trailer had been.

Back then.

A small, cramped aluminum trailer shaped like some zeppelin that was too heavy for flight.

If you looked carefully in daylight you could still see tiny holes in the ground where the thing had been parked.

The trailer.

All the nightmares flowed from there.

The shuttered windows. The bolted door. The crying.

And then the point beyond pain, the point of numbness, resignation—that place where all your expectations were linked to savagery.

He covered his face with his hands, and although he fought against it, he wept for a long time.

Rossiter lived alone in a run-down house in the northern part of Bristol, a house constructed on the side of a hill, a Victorian home that was one of the few in the district that hadn't been butchered into apartments. Christy parked her car on the sloping street and stared through the darkness at the pale light in a downstairs window. It was nine-thirty, perhaps a little too late to be making an unannounced call, a visit she wasn't sure about in any case. She tapped her fingers against the rim of the steering wheel and she thought: I really handled things badly, I really went at it with all the grace of a donkey in a glass factory. But how could she have anticipated Zachary's reaction, the look of pain on his face, the way he had hurried out of the house and into the darkness as if demons were pursuing him?

She had touched an exposed nerve, even if she wasn't certain of its exact location; she had touched it by blundering blindly into Zachary's fears. His fears, his secrets. Blundering, handling things like a crippled prize-fighter.

She got out of the car and walked up the driveway of Rossiter's house. From somewhere there was the smoky

155

perfume of a recent barbecue. She felt the touch of the night wind blowing against her hair. When she climbed up on the porch, she was startled by the sudden motion of a cat. She hesitated at the front door. What are you hiding, Zachary? Why are you so afraid? She raised a hand, pressed the doorbell.

When Rossiter appeared he was in his shirtsleeves, a cat cradled in each arm. He looked surprised and she thought she shouldn't have come here, but Rossiter knew this city, he knew its history, its politics, its scandals, with a recall more intimate and thorough than any information she might find in the morgue.

"My favorite reporter," he said. "What brings you out here?"

She stepped in and the aroma of cats was overwhelming. Rossiter led her into a living room, a place cluttered with books and more cats, at least four of them gazing at her from the sofa with feline hostility.

"If you can find a place to sit, good luck to you," he said. "Kick those cats off the couch or throw some of those papers on the floor." As he smiled at her she realized she was badly in need of some simple human warmth. She found a chair, sat down, took out a cigarette.

"I don't think I've ever seen you smoke before," he said.

"I never inhale."

"You're nervous about something. I've seen it for days."

She nodded and gazed at the cigarette in her hand. A woman takes her own life: it was the beginning and end of things—so why delve further? Simple. Your life is at stake here. The life you have carved out with Zachary is on the line, but you can't define that line, can't define the menace surrounding it, you only feel it crowding you. I am moving through a fog of perplexity, she thought, and I don't know where I'm going.

"Am I disturbing you?"

"Not remotely," Rossiter said.

She hesitated once more. "I need to ask you a couple of questions, that's all. I was in the morgue today looking up an obituary. A woman called Anthea McNair."

"And?"

"A suicide."

Rossiter took off his glasses. The cats leapt from his arms, blurs of glossy dark fur.

"Zachary's first wife," she said.

"I remember the incident."

"Do you?"

"Sure. I'm cursed with this impossible memory." He paused, gazing at the lenses of his glasses. "Why were you looking up this information anyhow?"

"Because I never knew about it until very recently—"

"You mean you didn't know about Anthea McNair when you married Zachary?"

She shook her head.

Rossiter rose and stood by the mantelpiece. He had the appearance of a badly creased sheet of paper. Crumpled, run-down, sagging. "I remember it quite well. It strikes me as a little strange that you were never told about it. I assumed you knew."

She suddenly remembered the way Rossiter had always vaguely disapproved of her marriage; it had to be because of the death of Anthea McNair—the stigma of suicide. Did he somehow imagine that Zachary had driven Anthea to her death?"

"I feel I'm a party to a concealment," he said.

"You didn't conceal anything. Zachary did."

"I wonder why." Rossiter put his glasses back on and peered at her, smiling in a way that suggested his concern for her. "I remember a reporter called Joe McMurtry who covered the suicide. He was before your time on the *Chronic*. A good reporter, but the kind of guy given to seeing conspiracies everywhere he looked. I think he lived his life in insane jealousy of those guys who covered Watergate. He wanted to be an investigative reporter, a hotshot."

Conspiracies, she thought. Such as?

Rossiter said, "He had the feeling he had only scratched the surface of Anthea McNair's death. He always felt there was something more to it."

"Like what?" Something beat at the back of her throat.

"I don't know, Christy."

"You must have some idea."

"The expression would be foul play."

"Foul play?"

"As in murder."

"That's absurd."

"I agree with you, Christy. But like I said, Watergate unhinged Joe more than a little. He was always looking for the dirt, always digging because he wanted to get his hands dirty."

It was too wild, she thought. Too crazy. This character McMurtry had been off the wall.

"Can I offer you a drink?" Rossiter asked.

She shook her head. "Where is McMurtry now?"

"Last I heard he was in Honolulu. Who knows where he is now? There was something of the Gypsy in Joe."

Christy leaned her head against the back of the chair and

turned the concept of murder over in her mind. No, it was going too far, it was going beyond the limit: Zachary would never have murdered his wife, he didn't have that kind of violence in him, he didn't have that sort of rage. She felt suddenly very tired, tired of digging, weary of questioning. But there were more questions and she wanted answers to them.

"The house I live in . . ."

"What about it? It's a white elephant, if you ask me."

"Do you know who lived there before?"

"Before what?"

"Before Zachary bought it."

Rossiter shook his head and said, "Somebody is keeping you in the dark, Christy."

"I don't know what you mean."

"It's always been the McNair house. For as long as I can remember it's always been in the family."

Christy felt something shift and turn and squirm inside her and for a moment she wished she hadn't come here.

"Your husband was probably raised in that house," Rossiter said.

Raised there, she thought.

Zachary raised there . . .

Which meant Leonora as well . . .

And then she remembered how Leonora had swept into the house as if it had belonged to her, and it suddenly made sense to her—but what didn't make any sense at all was why she hadn't been told. It would have been a perfectly natural thing for Zachary to mention something about his childhood memories, some association with the past, but he hadn't ever done that. Oh, Christ, there were too many secrets.

The paintings in the attic.

SM.

The M had to stand for McNair.

But what did the S stand for?

Her voice was feeble as she asked, "Do you know anything about the family?"

Rossiter shook his head. "Nothing."

She stood up, her legs cramped. The aroma of cats was overpowering her now, the stuffiness of the house getting to her.

"Leaving so soon?" Rossiter asked.

She nodded. "I better go. Thanks for your time. I appreciate it."

"I'm not sure that you do," he said, touching her hand gently. "If I can help, you know you only have to ask me, Christy."

Outside, she stood for a while on the porch and looked down across the lights of Bristol. Thousands of houses, thousands of secrets. Secrets and lies.

There had been too many lies, too many masks, too many trapdoors.

And she was falling through them into darkness, down and down into a place that was beginning to scare her.

Leonora stared from the window at the smoldering leaves. A thick plume of black smoke hung in the sky, drifting lazily upward toward the moon. She clutched the collar of her robe and pulled it against her neck. The big house was silent all around her; Daniel was already asleep, exhausted by their lovemaking. Asleep and happy, she thought, remembering the urgency with which he had held her, saying her name over and over, his energy surprising to her: he might have been a young man again, filled with vitality, consumed by the intensity of his love.

She turned from the window.

This is my room, she thought.

My room.

She looked at the sketches on the walls. Pen-and-ink sketches of kids. Kids change. They alter. They grow in other directions. And she felt a familiar sadness about the fact that nothing ever remained the same, that time passed in such a hasty blur. One had no control over time, except here in this room, where, after a fashion, she could freeze its motion.

Freeze it fast.

She walked toward a pile of old clothing and she bent down, picking up a plaid shirt which had been torn at the elbow long ago. Zachary had snagged the garment on the branch of a tree; he'd come crying to her the way he always did when something went wrong or when he was hurt, it was always her he came to because she had been the dead center of his universe, his only world, his love. And then there was a wool sweater he'd worn one bitter winter when there had hardly been any heat and the aluminum frame of the trailer had turned to ice and the nights had been long, darker than any she'd ever remembered. She recalled how she had held his body against hers through all the stark hours of dark. A bonding, a closeness, a relationship in blood that nobody could ever truly understand.

Nobody.

She let the sweater drop back on the pile and she thought she heard a slight noise outside the room. Maybe Daniel was prying again, snooping around the house. But then there was only silence. He had contaminated this place by entering it—how could he ever understand anything of the past? How could he ever know? There was a beautiful circle

161

and he was outside it, the way Christy was, the way Anthea had been—outsiders, looking in but never really seeing anything. Never really touching.

They thought they could belong. They thought they could find a point of entrance through marriage or friendship, but they never did.

She looked down at the pile of clothing again.

There were so many memories lying here. So many recollections of the past; sometimes she imagined that all she had were her memories, that her present life was simply some kind of dream, or the existence of somebody else she had somehow slipped into, the way one would put on a stranger's coat.

She let the palm of her hand rest against the soft wool of a garment and for a moment she'd gone back in time, back to where she could smell the clarity of scents—kerosene and candle wax and old food.

Kids grew, that was the trouble.

They grew, they developed their own ideas and they didn't come running every time they were in trouble. They imagined they could be independent, that they had lives outside the structure of the family—but that was only an illusion. There was nothing beyond the intricate bonds of a family, nothing at all. Everything was cold when you strayed beyond the bonds of blood.

She moved across the room and looked at a shelf that held various toys. Cheap toys. Broken toys. A monkey on a stick and a battered pack of cards and three lead soldiers from whose uniforms the paint had long since peeled. Cheap and broken, but they reminded her of love anyhow.

She picked up a wooden box, one of those boxes that had been used to hold cigars.

It rattled as she lifted it. On the lid was written the name Zack.

It might have held a collection of items to be used in some dark ceremony of witchcraft, things around which one wove spells, muttered incantations.

There were tiny teeth. A child's first teeth.

There were locks of dark brown hair.

These had all been Zachary's. These were her souvenirs of his boyhood.

She stared at them, remembering.

There was a catch at the back of her throat, a choking sensation.

And suddenly she realized she wanted to cry, something she hadn't done in years because tears always seemed to her such a waste of energy, such an indulgence. But there was a pain in her heart, a pain she didn't think she could stand.

Tears for the past. Tears for the immediate future. Tears because Zachary was going to be hurt again.

But it had to be done.

The family had to be made safe and secure, inviolate, beyond the intrusions of outsiders.

Poor dear Zachary.

11

Richie looked at his face in the bathroom mirror. His skin seemed jaundiced and there were tiny pouches under his eyes. You look sick, he thought, sick and old and tired. He splashed water over his face and went into the bedroom: Christ, he was sick of this goddamn hotel and sick of this city and what he had to do here. He was filled with a longing for a place without winters, a place without any past, where he might be free.

He lay back against the pillow and he wished the girl Samantha were here in the room with him now. He wanted sex, he wanted its sweet oblivion, losing himself in the secret folds of another body. And he turned his thoughts to Christy, wondering why she'd been so different from Anthea.

Anthea with her passions, her love letters—

Why was Christy so different? Her loyalty to Zachary, how could that be explained other than through the mysteries of love and loving? But he wasn't happy with the simply human chemistry of these matters.

You have to do it.

Leonora said you have to do it.

You have no choice in the matter.

He went to the telephone and dialed the number he had become so familiar with lately. A voice from the other end of the line said hello, a quick male voice, filled with anguish.

"Christy? Is that you?"

Richie said nothing for a long time. It was one-thirty A.M. *and nobody expected to get calls at that time of the day so it was strategically appropriate to keep silent, to make Zachary wonder if this was some ominous caller in the dead of night.*

"Christy?" *Zachary asked again.*

One-thirty A.M. *and Christy isn't home. Well well well. Richie said,* "Your wife out, Zack? Your wife out and playing around? Is that it?"

And he laughed.

"Who is this?" *Zachary asked.*

"You know me. Have you forgotten me already?"

The silence was long this time, long and alive with static, like there were gnats trapped inside the telephone wires.

Zachary said, "What do you want?"

"A few minutes of your time."

There was another silence and Richie thought: A few minutes of your time and the rest of your life as well.

She had been driving for a long time, not especially noticing where she was going, not especially caring—just driving the streets of Bristol aimlessly because she didn't want to go home yet, she didn't want to look at Zachary's face and think: He's a liar, my husband is a liar, it's all he seems to do. And it crossed her mind that maybe she was married to one of those pathological cases, a man who simply refused to tell the truth even when he could recognize it.

She drove through the quiet streets of old Bristol and then, fatigued by the city, oppressed by the buildings, she headed for the freeway, south for about twenty miles, seeing small factory towns on either side of the highway, foundries glowing in the darkness and great palls of gray smoke hanging in the half-moon sky. She saw the neon lights of motels—the Best Westerns and the Thrifty Inns and representatives of all the other chains that served the nightside of America. She thought about checking into one for the night, losing herself in the anonymity of registering, going inside a bland room and falling asleep on a bland bed—

Why couldn't you have been honest with me, Zack? Why couldn't you just have told me the simple truth?

She was sick to death of mysteries. She wanted a clean, open life, a life that wasn't wrapped in layers of misunderstandings and deceits and all the frustrations that went with them.

Twenty miles out of Bristol she drove off the freeway and reentered it northbound. She could see the electric haze of the city in the distance, as if it were a magnet light drawing her back. But goddammit, she wasn't ready to go back quite yet. And then ahead of her she saw a sign that said CRESTWICH 9M and she remembered that was where Leonora lived.

What could Leonora tell her? What did Zachary's sister know?

Leonora—but it was the wrong time of the night to go driving around looking for Leonora's house, crossing the county line and then waking the woman up and causing all kinds of inconvenience and making a nuisance of herself along the way.

But still . . .

Still . . .

The idea wouldn't go away, it wouldn't leave her mind.

Maybe Leonora could suggest some reason for all the lies. Maybe there was something—something stuck in the recesses of Zachary's childhood, say—that would explain all the subterfuge.

No, she thought, it's too late—

The hell it is, not when my whole marriage is at stake here.

The time of day wasn't an important issue when you were looking at the shape of the rest of your life, was it?

She drove until she came to a phone booth located outside an all-night laundromat and she parked the car, leaving the engine running, while she checked the directory. Leonora's married name was Huntington, Christy remembered, turning the thin pages quickly. She memorized the address. Crestwich was a dormitory for extremely affluent commuters, large houses located behind high walls, surrounded by ornate gardens and lush lawns and willow trees, a place whose atmosphere was rarefied; it was said that one needed an oxygen mask to breathe in Crestwich.

She got back inside the Jaguar and she thought: Mrs. Leonora Huntington won't exactly be thrilled by a visit at this time of the day, will she? Maybe she could postpone this trip until the morning, when things might look different—but how could they ever look any different than they did right now?

I don't give a damn whether she's over the moon about my visit or not. I'm going anyhow.

Then she was on the outskirts of Crestwich, where she first thought of turning back because suddenly this impulsive undertaking seemed ludicrous to her. No, dammit, I keep going. I've come this far so I'm going all the way—

Leonora. Anthea's enigmatic note. The real force/fear belongs to L.

She was looking for Mountjoy Drive now, which she found tucked away behind dense trees a mile from Main.

All the houses had huge wrought-iron gates and stout walls and sometimes pale lanterns burning over house numbers or name plates. The Willows. The Grange. The Meadows.

The Huntington home had no such name, just the number 33 embossed on a classy brassy plate. Christy went past it the first time, then swung the car around and returned, slowing as she reached the gates. I can't go in there. I can't.

She got out of the car, pushed the gates open and went up the driveway.

In the upper part of the house there was a light in a window. She thought she saw a shadow move behind the glass, but then it was gone and she wasn't sure if she'd really seen anything.

Then she stared.

At first she imagined a group of people had come out to meet her, but that wasn't what she was seeing at all—

She stared toward the entranceway where the four figures stood.

The same four figures that had been in all the paintings—

They loomed up over her, their blind eyes awkwardly seeking her out, their twisted limbs seeming to want to touch her, caress her. She backed off as if wounded, assailed all at once by the feeling that if she laid her fingers against

168

them they would come to life, transformed from stone into rancid flesh. ·

Four figures—

The same four figures—

And she was dizzy, as if overhead the black sky was caving in and the moon imploding, showering the night with silvery debris, the whole world inverted and flying away from her at a speed she could not calculate—and in this world there were no more coincidences, no more accidents, no more random workings of chance, this was a world of bizarre patterns, of illogical order, that made a special insane sense of its own.

The door behind her opened.

She swung around to see Leonora standing there, smiling.

Zachary kept imagining he heard the sound of the Jaguar in the driveway, but whenever he walked to the window there was nothing and he was left to wonder where she might be.

Left to wonder.

As he had been left to wonder before.

Alone in this house, suspecting the worst of all possible things.

He walked from one room to another, a man stalking something he could not quite define. Sometimes he would just stand at the window and look out into the blackness and think about what he might have lost out there.

Christy.

Which was when the pictures started to flood his mind, and with them a terrifying panic.

Christy and Richard. Dear God. No, not that, anything but that, he could take anything but that—

Christy and Richard and all those cheap rooms of sex and twisted sheets and ashtrays and the TV playing mindlessly to mute the noises of love—

He should have known it all along, right from the time when Rucker had mentioned a man, but his uncertainty then had been a necessary delusion.

Now she was out there in the night and all the things he had dreaded had come to pass.

He went inside his study and lay down on the sofa.

Christy. She loves me. She wouldn't love somebody else.

You thought the same thing about Anthea, didn't you?

You trusted.

Didn't you—

Christy lying somewhere with Richard and the past repeating like a voice trapped in a tunnel, destined to echo forever.

No. Give Christy the benefit of the doubt. Do that much at least.

He found this house insufferable. Outside, he sat on the steps, the door open at his back so that he might hear the telephone if it rang.

He waited. Off in the darkness he could see an occasional passing car, and each time he did, his heart moved inside his body, jumped a little. Christy, this is Christy coming home now.

He looked in the direction of the trees. What terrors did they conceal?

She isn't with Richard. She isn't with him at all.

He would have said so, he would have taken pleasure in saying so.

No, perhaps not, perhaps he would have found more pleasure in not saying so—

Zachary covered his face with his hands and he thought he might wait right here on these steps forever, the way he had waited—so long ago now—for Anthea.

"You're part of the family now, my dear, and of course you have every right to come here at any time, night or day, if something is troubling you," Leonora said. And she stroked the back of Christy's hand with fingertips that were warm. Christy looked past Leonora at the room they were seated in—a library with old leather-bound volumes and framed maps on the walls.

"You must feel free to talk with me, Christy. You know that, don't you?"

Christy smiled in a tired way, nodding her head. "I'm worried about Zachary," she said.

"And what has he been up to?" Leonora's expression was that of a governess fondly accustomed to the misbehavior of small boys.

"I guess it's more like what he hasn't been up to. You'd call them lies of omission, I guess."

"Such as?" Leonora reached out and gently smoothed a strand of hair from Christy's forehead.

"There was Anthea—"

"And he hadn't told you about her?"

"No." Christy looked down at the floor. "I hadn't heard about her until I met you."

"Don't you think it's perfectly understandable, my dear?"—and Leonora spread her hands out in a gesture of absolution. "He marries after a terrible tragedy. He is not happy about the prospect of causing his lovely new bride any concern. He wants, naturally, to forget. Why linger in this past, after all? He loves you, Christy. Why would he trouble you, upset you with his past sorrows?"

Christy stared at Leonora's face; she was beautiful in a way that suggested great care had been taken of her complexion and hair. Expensive care. And just for a moment she reminded Christy of something that had been lovingly preserved. Okay, she thought. Give that point to Zachary and go on to the next. "He also neglected to mention the fact that Anthea had lived and died in the same house—"

Leonora laughed, a tiny, condescending sound. And then she reached over and took both of Christy's hands in her own. "I'm sure he just didn't want you to feel bad about your home, that's all. Why would he give you feelings of uneasiness?"

Christy thought: What is this? The Zachary McNair Protection Society? But what would you have expected in any case?—it was perfectly natural for a sister to be forgiving of her brother's weaknesses and lies. Christy rose and walked around the room, conscious of Leonora's eyes following her. I am uneasy, she told herself. Leonora has an answer for everything and that makes me itch. "Why did Anthea kill herself?"

"I am not hiding anything when I tell you, my dear, that she was a rather secretive creature given to melancholy. Between ourselves"—and Leonora leaned forward, looking conspiratorial—"I think she was not right for Zachary in the way that you obviously are."

She is too nice. Everything is too wonderful. Christy paused by the desk and stared at the gleaming wood. "Why didn't Zachary tell me that the house we live in has been in the McNair family for years? Why didn't he tell me that it's the house where he was raised?"

Leonora smiled and Christy saw something small and

shadowy flicker across her face, a faint unease. "You surprise me. Are you saying he never mentioned this to you?"

"That's right."

Leonora seemed to drift off into a private space, where she found something pleasurable; her eyes glossed over. Christy had the odd impression that Leonora was always about to spring, like some black cat. And then something else seized her attention, the feeling that there was somebody on the other side of the library door. She hadn't exactly heard anything, but she knew that somebody was out there listening.

"I can't explain why he'd fail to bring up this subject, Christy."

"It's not only the house. He never mentions his family. His mother, his father—"

"Our mother died in childbirth. Zachary never knew her. Our father died sometime later. There isn't much to tell about either of them, Christy."

"Childbirth?"

"Giving birth to Zachary, my dear."

Christy let this snippet of information sink through her weary brain; she looked at her watch. It was two-thirty. She badly wanted to go home and sleep now. Giving birth to Zachary . . . She said, "I noticed the statues outside the house."

"Ah, yes. Aren't they intriguing?"

"Who is SM?"

"SM?"

"The sculptor—"

"I'm sure I don't know."

Christy wanted to say: You're lying, this is all some

173

awful charade we're going through, but she felt paralyzed by Leonora's confidence.

"It's just that I found some canvases in our attic, done by the same person who sculpted those statues—" she finally said.

"Are you sure?"

"Positive—"

"Then you might have quite a windfall coming to you. They're probably worth some money. That's a coincidence, isn't it?"

Christy was tempted to say something about the amazing elasticity of coincidence and how far you could stretch it, but once again she didn't speak. Leonora, politely covering a yawn, rose from her chair. "I'm very tired, my dear. But I have enjoyed our little talk and I hope I've put your mind at rest—"

And then they were out in the hallway. Empty. There was nobody listening, nobody eavesdropping. Leonora walked with her to the front door, opening it for her. The night air was chilly, the statues grotesque. (They're waiting for something, Christy thought. Something or somebody. And she shivered a little.)

"If you're too tired, I'll get my driver to take you," Leonora said.

"I'm fine, Leonora. Really. And thanks. Thanks for your time."

"We must do it again. At a civilized hour, of course," and Leonora reached out, hugging her, pressing a firm kiss against her lips before she stepped back inside.

Christy went down the steps.

I'm fine, Leonora. Sure, I'm fine.

I know you're lying. And that makes me just wonderful.

But what did the lies add up to? What in the name of God did they conceal?

And she was scared now, scared because subterfuge and concealment had become conditions of her life. Because it seemed to her that the whole surface of her life had simply cracked open and that in the fissures beneath her she could see only shadows move. Shadows that were rising upward like creatures lain long dormant seeking freedom . . .

Freedom to do what?

She listened to the sound of her feet on the gravel path as she saw the front gates come in sight.

And then she jumped back, sucking cold night air into her lungs—

The figure of a man had stepped out in front of her from nowhere.

And she must have moaned in fear and surprise because she could hear an echo of her own voice inside her head.

"Mrs. McNair, I'm sorry, I didn't mean to startle you. My name is Daniel Huntington," and he held out his hand. He was short, his skull stripped of hair, and he wore a thick striped robe; his face was sunk in weariness.

"You surprised me," Christy said. Scared me to death, actually, she thought, looking at the apparition in front of her, unable to imagine a marriage between this man and Leonora.

"I apologize. I'm not in the habit of running around at this time of night in a robe, I assure you."

He spoke in the modulated tones of a man of some education and background, with a definite firmness to his voice, as if somewhere in his life he had been accustomed to getting his own way. She couldn't imagine him winning even the smallest of victories over Leonora.

He said, "I overheard some of your conversation with my wife." Daniel Huntington looked toward the house as if he was afraid of being seen; his glance was wary. "I must ask you not to come here again, Mrs. McNair."

"Why?"

"I think you put a certain stress on my wife—"

"Stress?"

He nodded his head. "I love Leonora very much," he said. "She is a very special person in many ways."

Christy saw her breath hang on the air. "Is this some kind of warning, Mr. Huntington?"

He smiled. "A warning?" He raised one hand in the air and for one dreadful moment she thought she was going to be struck by this man. What was Daniel Huntington trying to tell her?

"Her family is very important to her, Mrs. McNair."

"I gathered that much—"

"She lives at times in the past, you understand. The past is like a private retreat for her. Sometimes the past is sacred to certain people," he said. "Sometimes they need to preserve it intact. Old family loyalties. Old longings. I'm sure you understand."

Christy shook her head. "I don't understand at all." Puzzles, more conundrums peddled in the night like locked boxes you couldn't open. Why didn't anybody ever come out with the truth? Why was it always sleight-of-hand and silk handkerchiefs from sleeves and trick decks of cards? I only want the truth, she thought. I only want to repair my marriage, if I can.

Daniel Huntington was silent for a moment, looking back at the house. "I wouldn't like anything to happen to Leonora," he said. A pause, a beat. "And I wouldn't like anything to happen to you either."

"Meaning what?" she asked.

But he was moving past her in the direction of the house now, his robe flapping at his ankles.

"Meaning what?" she called after him.

He paused and turned around, and even in the darkness she could see his weary face and the manner in which his body slumped. "Go away somewhere. Get away, Mrs. McNair. Go anywhere. Leave this family." He paused once more, and when he next spoke his voice was a whisper. "I married very late in life, Mrs. McNair, which is not always the best thing to do. One has feelings of love that are almost adolescent in their intensity. It's too late for me to leave Leonora, you understand? But——" He stopped, as if afraid that he had said too much. "If I were younger, if I were stronger, I might simply walk away."

She watched him climb the steps toward the statues, saw the door open, then close behind him, and then the night wind was rising again, making the leaves whisper all around her like small but shrill voices speaking—as Daniel Huntington had done—in a language she did not understand.

12

Leon Coldwind's heart was beating a little too fast inside his chest for comfort. He had experienced similar palpitations of a minor kind in the past, never anything serious—thankfully—but this had been happening all morning long, ever since he had looked at his appointment book and noticed that his secretary, Della, had scheduled an eleven-thirty appointment with somebody called Christy McNair. McNair.

He turned the name over in his mind a couple of times, wondering how he might extricate himself from the meeting. There was always some slight possibility, of course, that this McNair was not related to the family he knew and whose affairs he had long administered, but at the same time the name filled him with a sense of unhappiness and guilt. Every lawyer, he thought, is a mercenary at heart, and he was no exception—but as he stood at the window of his office and looked into the rainy bluster of Manhattan he experienced a sense of some sorrow that his earlier idealism had been replaced by a definite eye for the bank balance.

He removed a small nail clipper from the pocket of his

vest and began to file away at his fingernails. The clock on his desk said eleven-twenty-three.

Christy McNair.

He tried to control himself. And then he was thinking about Leonora Huntington. Go back a few years, he told himself. Go back to when you were not a partner in a middle-sized Manhattan law firm, turn the springs of the old timepiece back and remember your own youthful desperation.

Ah, yes. There are always excuses.

Clients often do dark deeds. Most of them we do not know about and do not care to uncover. But this . . .

The hopeless heart. The yearning for Leonora's body. The youthful urge, the sounds of love chiming inside the head. Back when the blood was bold. Now, ruefully, he wondered what Leonora was like in bed and he felt resentment that he had never known her, that Old Moneybags Huntington was the one who had staked a claim on that territory.

There was a tap on his office door.

And his heartbeat was faster than that of a hare cornered by hounds.

He cleared his throat and said, "Come in," and the door was opened by Della, who was followed by a good-looking young woman who had to be Christy McNair. She smiled sweetly and entered the office, wearing a raincoat and carrying a matching purse, looking perfectly splendid.

"Mrs. McNair?" he said, watching Della withdraw in her familiar stooped manner.

The woman nodded.

"Ah," and he gestured toward a chair, watching her sit down. He put the tips of his fingers together and placed them against his lips. "What can I do for you?"

"I'm a journalist, Mr. Coldwind," she said. "I work for the *Bristol Chronicle*."

"Bristol? Nice town," he said, and he felt his heart turn over. McNair, Bristol—these two names congealed in his mind. She is one of the Bristol McNairs, he thought, and he pictured Leonora again and was filled with dread. "What kind of things do you write about?"

She smiled and he thought: She has a good face, a strong face; one could see a certain determination in her features.

"I write the social column," she said.

"I see." He picked up his silver fountain pen and rolled it between his fingers. The social column, he thought, and he wondered where this was going to lead. He found himself gazing at the window a moment; rain was slithering down the glass.

"I was in an art gallery in Bristol recently and I saw a rather powerful painting by someone who called himself SM—"

SM, he thought.

SM.

The two letters had the sound of soft footsteps coming after him. Soft, dreadful.

"I want to interview the artist, write something about him, and it's my understanding that you represent him," the woman said, leaning forward in her chair.

Coldwind glanced at the shelves of lawbooks, great tomes bound in leather. You could try to hide in the pages of those books but somebody would always catch you. SM. "I do represent the artist," he said, and his voice was thin.

"Then you can arrange a meeting?" the woman asked.

He stood up now. "Unhappily, the person in question passed on some time ago." Passed on, he thought. The cheerful euphemism. Passed on indeed. He looked at Mrs. McNair and wondered if she believed him or if she thought he was just another lawyer protecting a client.

"Oh," she said, disappointed. "That's really too bad. I wonder if you might give me some idea of his identity then—my readers might be interested."

No, he thought. But I can tell you where he might be found, my dear young woman. I could tell you that. He said, "I'm afraid we lawyers operate under the principle of confidentiality, Mrs. McNair. I'm not at liberty to say anything."

"I understand," she said. She had sharp, intelligent eyes, and he didn't enjoy the feeling of being trapped in her look. "Perhaps you could answer this for me, Mr. Coldwind. Was his last name the same as my own?"

"I'm sorry, I wish I could help—"

"What are you hiding?" she asked suddenly. "What is everybody hiding, Mr. Coldwind?"

He smiled. There was a measure of desperation in the way she asked her questions—and he, for his sins, had always been a sucker for a desperate woman. If she were suddenly to cry, he thought, he would tell her anything she needed to know. "I am not hiding anything," he said.

She stood up, her hands clenched at her side.

"You must understand, Mrs. McNair. I have my duty to my client."

"Duty," she said, as if the words were beyond her comprehension. "Thanks for your time anyhow. I appreciate it."

He walked with her toward the door, thinking: I do not altogether care for myself. There are dark moments in my heart now and then.

He took her hand and shook it, looking into her eyes and seeing something that could only be fear.

In the street the wind had died a little but it was still raining and the sidewalks were scattered with puddles. SM is dead, Christy thought. Long live SM. Why did she know Coldwind wasn't telling the truth? Hiding behind his professional veneer?

You've been around lies long enough to recognize them.

She turned up the collar of her coat. Lawyers and priests, she thought, they give nothing away. She should have know better.

On the corner of Seventh Avenue and Fortieth Street she paused a moment, uncertain of her direction. And suddenly she was remembering her odd conversation with Daniel Huntington, which now had the shimmery quality of a dream. What had he been trying to tell her anyhow? She wasn't sure. You're not sure of anything these days, Christy. Rain, swept by a sudden gust of wind, blew against her face.

Last night, when she'd arrived home, she'd found Zachary asleep on the sofa, and this morning there had been a note on the kitchen table which very simply said:

Glad you came home.

Love,
Z

There had been something forlorn in the note that had touched her. Now she wished she'd wakened him last night and made love to him, as if through the act of sex they could put aside all the lies and the obscurities, and go on with the business of their marriage.

Maybe she would go to his office right now, surprise him, make him buy her lunch. Maybe. But what would she say to him if she did? It would be a lunch fraught with sharp silences, things unsaid and perhaps unsayable, words you couldn't spit out, like little fragments of splintered bone you got between your teeth.

She headed north anyhow, the wind at her back.

A wasted day, she thought.

I might as well go home.

I might as well go back to the mysteries.

But then she realized she was across the street from the offices of Dackson, McNair; she looked toward the entranceway, where a few office girls were standing around in raincoats, huddled against the weather.

She shrugged. Okay, go see Zachary.

She was about to step from the sidewalk and go across the damp street when she froze. She froze, couldn't move.

She saw Zachary come out and move toward the steps.

Somebody was with him.

Alongside him.

Zachary turned his face and said something to the man and they walked together along the sidewalk away from her, and she turned her face to see them disappear around the corner, her husband and the man she knew as Richie, strolling together as if they had some common purpose, some common destination.

She turned her face upward to the sky.

Clouds swirled against the towers of the city, and the rain, with a renewed vitality, began to batter her upturned face.

Lenora could feel her husband's eyes watching her. It seemed to her that whenever she happened to turn her face in his direction, he was following her with those tight little eyes of his. It was something she had been conscious of ever since the night he'd gone to her room, and she didn't like it—it made her uneasy, as if she were a patient in a terminal ward guarded by a fastidious nurse.

He raised his face from his luncheon and asked, "Is something troubling you?"

"No," she answered. "Why do you ask?"

He shrugged and put his fork down alongside his half-eaten plate. "It's just that you look worried, my dear. Has it got something to do with Leon Coldwind?"

"What has Leon Coldwind got to do with anything?"

"He just telephoned you, didn't he?"

"What is this? Have you started to listen in on my phone calls, Daniel? Have you started to eavesdrop on me? First you go to my room, now you listen in on extension phones. My God, what next?"

She got up from the table quickly and left the dining room. She entered the library, where she sat down in a chair at the window and tugged at the string of pearls she wore around her neck. All morning long there had been cumbersome, swollen rainclouds in the sky and now, at last, a few drops had begun to fall across the lawn and the dying flowerbeds. She clenched her hand, made it a fist, put it against her forehead. Leon Coldwind, she thought.

Christy had visited Coldwind, asking questions. She had actually gone there as if she had some right to know anything.

Just as she had had the temerity to come here last night with her interrogative manner.

Leonora bit her lower lip and experienced one of those moments that were rare in her life, an unfamiliar sense of her discipline breaking into fragments inside her, a yielding in some deep place, a corrosion of her will.

She rose from her chair and she paced the room thinking, thinking.

Why did this one have to be difficult where Anthea had been easy?

Why had Zachary chosen a woman with some willpower, some tenacity?

She stopped at the window. How much does she know anyhow? Of course, Coldwind was a whore and his price had been paid and he would have all the discretion of a high-rent callgirl—she was not worried about the little lawyer at all. No, she was only concerned about Christy and the way she just kept going after answers when there were no answers to which she was entitled.

The door of the library opened.

"Are you all right?" Daniel asked.

She didn't answer him.

"I love you," he said.

She didn't move, didn't speak.

"You know that, don't you?"

She felt her husband's lips press against the back of her neck and she shifted slightly away.

"What's the matter?" he asked.

She turned around and stared at him. "There are certain things you could never understand."

"Try me," he said.

"Try you?" and she laughed.

"Tell me about your family." There was an imploring note in his voice. Tell me, tell me, let me understand, take me inside the sacred circle and allow me to become a member. Please do that much for me.

"I never speak about my family," she said.

"But they're always near, aren't they? They're always close to you, Leonora, always somewhere in your thoughts."

"What would you know about family?" she asked.

"Explain it to me, Leonora. Make me understand. Make me understand why you keep all those things in your room—"

My room, she thought. Then he had seen more than she imagined. She said, "You'll always be a stranger, Daniel. You'll never be any more than that."

And she could see how much that stung him, the way his face crumpled, the trembling of his lip. For a second she felt sorry for him.

He was silent for a moment and then he said, "The young woman who was here last night. She's a problem to you, isn't she?"

Leonora shrugged her shoulders lightly.

"She's a nuisance, Leonora. Isn't that what she is?"

"Yes," she said. "A nuisance."

"And a threat?"

A threat? she wondered. Nobody is ever a threat to me. Nobody has that kind of power.

"If you like that word, Daniel," she said.

"I don't like anything that might harm you," he said.

Leonora walked across the room, tugging once again at her string of pearls. A threat, she thought again.

"Nothing is going to harm me, Daniel."

He gazed at her, his shoulders hunched, his whole body sagging. "How can you be sure of that?" he asked.

Smiling a little, she answered, "I can be sure of almost anything when I want to be."

She walked toward the stairs.

She would go up to her room.

She would step inside and lock the door and think of how the living might die so that the secrets of the dead could be preserved—

And she would think of Christy, as if she were remorselessly sticking pins into a tiny wax effigy of Zachary's wife.

It was one of those midtown bars filled with lean girls with frightened hairstyles and young men who clutched portfolios as if their lives depended on them. The advertising set, Zachary thought, hunched over his gin and tonic and feeling quite miserable, uneasy in a setting such as this, where a superficial grace and an awareness of fashion were the only real currency for belonging. He sipped his drink, then set it aside and turned to glance at Richard. Beautiful as ever, he thought. Just as beautiful as he had always been, the features symmetrical and flawless, the eyes dazzling. The eyes, Zachary had often thought, of a mesmerist. He looked away because suddenly he was thinking of Anthea being drawn into those eyes, drawn down and down to a place where she no longer understood who she was, where her identity became as splintered as old wood.

He looked at Richard's long tapered fingers; refined, artistic, sensitive. He could imagine those fingers moving in the private places of Anthea's body, skin upon skin, whorls tracing the line of the spine or gently massaging the shoulders or lingering between the thighs.

He looked away from Richard now because he couldn't keep old pains from his eyes, couldn't look at him without feeling a defensive glaze go across his expression. Richard, he wanted to ask, why? Why Anthea of all people? And then he felt he was tumbling down some long, greasy slide and that there was nothing at the bottom to catch him. He stared across the bar where a gorgeous girl in a red jacket and tight velour pants was posing, twisting her head this way and that as if to afford the common rabble a chance to study her beauty, "Your health, Zachary," Richard said, raising his rum and Coke, the color of very old blood.

Zachary didn't speak. Your health, he thought. He didn't give a damn about Richard's health. How could he? What was he supposed to do, kiss the man, embrace him, tell him that all had been forgiven long ago?

"How have you been, Zachary?"

Zachary shrugged. "Was Christy with you last night?" he asked, a question he didn't want answered.

"She's different from Anthea," Richard said.

Zachary turned away from the other man: there were times when he was too handsome to look at, because those times evoked the way Anthea had been attracted to him. But he wasn't concerned about Anthea now, he was thinking of Christy, wondering where she had been last night. But he didn't have to wonder, did he? Because he knew.

He knew only too well.

"How long have you been seeing her?" His throat was dry and his palms itched.

"A few weeks, Zack. Long enough."

Zachary could feel the jagged pain around his heart; Christy just couldn't, she couldn't, she wouldn't enter into any affair with Richard. But then, he'd thought the same thing about Anthea and he'd been very wrong—he had never been more wrong in his life.

"Long enough for what?" Zachary asked. He wanted to remain numb and indifferent and not feel these awful claws tearing at his heart like this.

"She's good, Zachary. She's very good. She's better than Anthea. She's more demonstrative. More passionate."

"I don't believe any of this, I don't believe a goddamn word of it," Zachary said, conscious of his voice rising, aware of people in the bar staring at him as if he were some curiosity.

"I don't care what you believe," Richard said, and sipped his drink. "I know the truth about your beloved Christy. I know her better than you."

Zachary reached out and gripped the lapels of Richard's coat.

"I hate you, Richard. I think I hate you more than any person alive. You killed Anthea—"

"She killed herself, didn't she?"

"You might just as well have plunged the knife into her wrists," Zachary said. "And now you want Christy?"

"You've got it the wrong way around, Zack. Christy wants me."

"No—"

"You want times, locations, you want to know all the gruesome details?"

Zachary clutched the glass so hard in the palm of his hand that it snapped. Broken pieces were scattered across the table.

"Clumsy, Zack. Always clumsy."

"I don't believe a goddamn word you're saying, Richard. I just don't believe any of it. Christy wouldn't—"

"You don't know your wife, friend. You haven't ever really touched her, have you?"

189

"She loves me. I love her."

"Pathetic, Zack. Love has nothing to do with what Christy and I have in common. I'm talking about lust."

Suddenly Zachary was on a downward course into mad jealousy, creating perverse icons in his mind, seeing Christy straddling this man, her expression one of abandon, her eyes wild, her hair falling over her naked back and her thighs moving from side to side as she sat on top. And the possibility of this kind of intimacy shattered him, broke him into tiny pieces.

"Why?" he asked. "Why are you trying to destroy this marriage too?"

Richard smiled. "You know why. I don't need to answer that, do I?"

Christy returned to Bristol in the middle of the afternoon on a train that was virtually empty save for a few women carrying shopping bags with names like Saks and Bloomingdale's on them. She sat at the window, watching New York City slip away, thinning out into suburbs that finally yielded to green fields and scattered towns. But she wasn't really seeing any of this, she wasn't seeing anything at all.

She sat with her head back against the seat and she thought about Zachary and Richie together—there had to be a relatively simple explanation, but how many times had she sought reasonable answers, only to find a deck filled with nothing but jokers?

Zachary and Richie. What was it about those two? What did they have in common?

When she got off the train she went inside the station snack bar and drank weak coffee, smoking one cigarette after another. She had time to kill before Zachary's train. Time to kill and nothing to do but feel lost, as if somewhere along the way her compass had malfunctioned and her maps were shredded to pieces and the stars in the sky had changed positions. Dear God. Zachary and Richie.

She went outside and walked up and down the platform. When Zachary's train arrived, she watched him disembark, and for a moment she was tempted to hide, to duck out of sight. Tempted to turn her back and walk away; instead she went to him and embraced him quickly and they walked arm in arm out to the Jaguar in the parking lot. Richie, she thought. She had to find some way to raise the subject.

They got in the car and she backed it out of the lot into the street. He was silent, grim, his face shadowy, his eyes distant. She could see that he was in one of his unreachable moods. One of his retreats. And what she wondered, with a sense of acute loss, was where the man she'd married had gone. Where he'd disappeared to.

"I was in town today," she said.

"Manhattan?"

She nodded.

"Why didn't you come to the office?"

"I was going to—then I saw you come out of the building with a man and I didn't want to intrude—"

"Did you recognize the man I was with?"

She hesitated. Tact, circumspection, finding the right phrases. "I think I've seen him around town."

"Around town?" Zachary had gripped her arm. "I'm not surprised to hear that, Christy. I mean, you've had drinks with him. You've been meeting him. I'd say he was a pretty close friend of yours."

191

"A close friend? Why do you think that?"

Zachary let his hand fall from her arm and she glanced at him—there was a look of hurt on his face such as she'd never seen before. She wanted to reach out, console him somehow, soothe the pain.

"How often do you see him anyhow?"

She shook her head. She could feel it coming, a major accusation, something she just couldn't take.

"You and him get together, don't you? Afternoons, it must be pretty intimate, you must spend a lot of time in hotel rooms—"

"Zachary, for Christ's sake, I once had a drink with the man. I don't particularly like him and I have not been to any hotel room with him!"

He was silent, slumped in his seat, staring out moodily at the passing street. Where had he dug up this stuff? Had Richie made some outrageous claims? What else could it have been?

She said, "Love, I hardly know him. I ran into him at a couple of social events but beyond that I don't know the first thing about him."

Zachary spoke in a voice that was low, almost inaudible. "He was Anthea's lover. That's who he was, Christy. Anthea's great passion."

She turned to Zachary. Anthea's lover—Anthea and Richie—

How could that be—

"Didn't you know that much, Christy?"

"No," she said. "No, I didn't."

"You know his name, don't you?"

"Only his first name. Only Richie—"

192

"Not his last? You don't know his last?"

She shook her head. Something was coming in at her, something dark and dreadful, something she didn't want to encounter—

There was an odd smile on Zachary's face.

"It's the same as your own, Christy. It's McNair."

"McNair?"

"Richard McNair."

"Is he—" A question slipped out of her mind. Something she didn't want to ask.

She felt her knuckles go tight on the steering wheel. Richard McNair . . .

Zachary looked at her. "He's my brother," he said.

It was too complex now, it was too difficult to grasp, this was suddenly more than some simple skeleton in the family history, more than just dried-out old bones and fine dust. But what? Exactly what?

His brother, Richie.

And Richie had been Anthea's love.

Richie, Richie, what kind of man was it who stole and seduced his brother's wife?

And—

and I was going to be next—

After Anthea, Christy.

I was supposed to succumb and fall into a hopelessly passionate love affair with Richie. I was to be his next conquest.

His next triumph.

Next victim.

And for what? for what possible reason?

What conceivable purpose?

193

She stared through the window of the car at streets that should have been familiar to her.

But they had been stripped of that quality.

They were alien to her now.

As alien, as foreign, as everything else in her life.

13

"If that's what he told you, he was lying to you, Zachary. If he said there was some kind of sexual relationship between us, he wasn't telling you the truth." Christy stared at her husband, then down at the cigarette smoldering in the ashtray. "For one thing, I'm hurt that you'd believe him rather than me. For another, I'm beginning to wonder if lying is something that runs through your entire family. I can't think of an instance when I've been told the truth by any one of you. . . ." She looked at Zachary's face—what in the name of God was that expression there and why did it frighten her so much? She shut her eyes to think her way beyond the entire fabric of deceit, to find a clearing where there might be bright daylight and no shadows, a place where nothing could hide or be hidden.

Zachary didn't say anything.

"Why would Richie want Anthea? And why me, Zachary? Why would he want me to become Anthea's successor? I mean, what is it about your whole family that doesn't add up in any way I can make sense of?" Worst of all was that she, who had been consistently lied to, was now the one who was mistrusted; a world turned upside down with a bang. "Jesus Christ, Zachary. There's only one thing that's stopping me from going upstairs and packing my suitcase and kissing you off once and for all—and that's the simple fact that I love you. I love you, Zachary, despite everything. Can't you get that through your thick head?"

Zachary rose from his chair. "He took Anthea away from me, Christy. He took her away . . . and then he said he'd taken you away as well."

"But I'm still here!" and she sighed, because she couldn't see any way to get through to her own husband now. "You never even mentioned you had a brother. The same way you never mentioned Leonora to me. Is there an army of McNairs lying around the place, Zack? Is it something like that?"

"I didn't mention him because it hurt me to think about him and it still hurts me."

Christy walked over to him and laid her hands against his shoulders. "You still don't believe me, do you, Zack? You'd still rather believe your brother, wouldn't you?"

He shook his head very slowly.

"Why does Richie want to hurt you, Zachary? Why would your own brother want to do such a thing? Does he get his thrills from bringing pain into people's lives?"

There were tiny nerves working across Zachary's face, an elaborate network of threads she thought was slowly coming undone.

"Love," she said. "I don't know how to put this any more clearly for you. Your brother and I did not go to bed with each other. We never even embraced, for Christ's sake. He's a very handsome man, but you've overlooked my own private morality here. I'm not going to deny I found him

196

attractive—but there's a whole world of difference between being attracted to somebody and actually doing something about it."

God, she was tired. Tired, perplexed. And afraid still, as if out of the shadows of all the little mysteries there were other, darker creatures about to emerge; she didn't think she had the strength to encounter any of them.

"Keep it in mind, Zachary. I love you."

As she watched his doubting, she wondered why he would believe his brother so unreservedly—as if Richie had some hold over him. A hold, she thought—here was a whole family with inscrutable holds over each other, as if somewhere in the dim past impossible bargains had been forged and nothing, nothing at all, could snap those chains.

She lit another cigarette and the smoke stung her throat.

"I assume Anthea killed herself because your sweet sibling Richie drove her to it. Am I right?"

It was the wrong question to ask. She saw a tremor of pain cross his face and she wished she hadn't asked anything so obviously hurtful to him.

"Forget it," she said. Now the other question, the other one she needed to ask, and suddenly it didn't matter a damn if he didn't have the courage to answer it. "Why was Richie here on the night of her death, Zachary?"

He raised his face to look at her and she could still see a whole series of doubts in his expression.

"Well? Why was he here that night?"

"I don't remember."

"I'm tired of the bullshit, Zack. I'm up to here in the stuff and it's rising fast enough to suffocate me."

He stood up, the expression on his face troubled, distant, and she had the feeling he was sifting through Richie's lies

197

all over again. What on earth had Richie said? I screwed your wife, Zachary. She and I spent delicious hours doing it like crazy. She's like a beast in heat.

Had it been something like that? Had Richie used those kinds of words to Zachary, or had it been something more subtle?

"Why was he here, Zachary? Why was your wife's lover here that night?"

"I don't . . ."

She crushed her unsmoked cigarette angrily. You can take only so much, she thought. You can't take anything beyond a certain level because you've just about had it.

"Did you and he have an argument? Was that it? While you were arguing, did poor little Anthea go upstairs to take her own life, was it something like that?"

God, she wanted to hold him and make him feel all right, make him feel safe, but she wasn't going to give in to any display of affection until she'd had some satisfactory answers.

He poured himself a glass of Scotch, which he drank thirstily, and then he refilled the empty glass.

He said, "She used to write him these love letters. The saddest things I ever read. It was as if Anthea was living through an adolescence she'd missed the first time around. Maybe it was worse than that—maybe Richie provided something that I was incapable of. She was forever writing little fragments of romantic poems and leaving them lying around. But I never gave that very much thought until one day I saw them together. I actually spied on them." Zachary sipped his drink, paused a moment. "A fine and wonderful thing, don't you think? Spying on your own wife? What kind of man does that, Christy?"

"A very insecure, jealous man, I guess."

"You guess correctly, of course. Anyhow, I imagined it would be a passing phase. Then . . . Then . . ." A terrible look crossed his face. "I came home here one day early. I didn't realize the house wasn't empty. Can you guess the rest of that little episode, Christy?"

She looked away from him. She knew what was coming.

"You walk in through the front door and for a moment everything seems fine, nothing is out of place. Slowly, in a way you can't understand, you realize something is wrong. You don't want to believe it, of course. But something in your heart tells you that you're horribly correct and so you climb the stairs and you stop outside the bedroom door because you hear . . . you hear whispers . . . you hear certain unmistakable sounds and through a gap in the door you see something that shocks you and you recognize, in one awful flash, the true nature of human betrayal, Christy. You freeze because all your volition vanishes. You don't do anything. You just leave. You go back downstairs and out of the house and after that several hours are lost, a whole sequence of time just blacked out. Lost to you forever."

He stopped, staring into his glass.

"This was my brother we're talking about. My brother and my wife."

But what happened next? What happened after that on the night of her death?

Zachary said, "I must have driven around for hours, I don't remember, I can't really say where I might have gone. Then I came home. Richard was sitting right here in this room. Alone."

"And where was Anthea?"

"Upstairs. I thought she was taking a bath."

"And?"

"It wasn't what she was doing, Christy. It wasn't what she was doing at all. I went upstairs to the bathroom. The rest you know, don't you?"

No, she thought, I don't know the rest.

I don't really know the rest at all.

And suddenly she was thinking of something Rossiter had told her about the old newspaperman McMurtry and his suspicions concerning the suicide of Anthea McNair. But no, wait, don't let your imagination transport you in any such direction, don't get carried away in the foaming slipstream of suspicion. Anthea McNair killed herself because of an unrequited love, because she'd seen no future in her passion for Richard, that was why she'd done it, that was the only reason, nothing else at all. Dear God, what else could have happened in any case?

You can imagine the poor woman devoted to the beautiful Richie.

You could imagine him trying to get rid of her, use her until he was tired of her, you could hear the sound of her big romantic dreams just breaking apart and then the only course left to her had been the blades through the wrists, the terrible cutting steel—that was how it had happened.

And then Richie, having successfully driven Anthea out of Zachary's life, had tried to drive a similar wedge between Christy and her husband—and that was where the puzzles really deepened, that was where there was a kind of crossroads of conundrums.

Richie sits down here in the study while Anthea lies in the bathtub bleeding to death. Leaving behind her sad scribblings. Her enigmatic little phrases.

. . . But I don't see how I can get out of this alive.

What was she referring to when she'd written that sorrowful phrase?

All the pictures swirling through Christy's head were misty and dark.

Why, Richie?

Why do you want to take Zachary's women away from him like this?

And then she was thinking of his beautiful face and his slender body, but it was no longer anything she found attractive—instead it was rotten, a worm turning, a maggot twisting at the very heart of a rose.

Richie.

And Leonora, where did Leonora fit in all of this?

Why had Leonora never mentioned Richie?

This house, this haunted house, how many things had happened within these walls, how many unhappy specters rattled on moonless nights!

Zachary came and stood beside her. "Christy?" And he looked at her questioningly.

She said, "I know what you're going to ask. My answer's the same as before, Zachary. I had nothing to do with your brother. I had nothing to do with him at all. The only thing I grasp is that he wants to hurt you, and I don't know why. Do you?"

Zachary stared out of the window, said nothing.

Something he can't bring himself to speak about even now.

A barrier too thick.

"Tell me something," she said. "Who is SM? Who is the painter, Zack?" And she thought: Don't keep lying to me, don't keep being evasive. Just say the truth.

He shrugged. "I honestly don't remember," and she

realized he was using the word honestly as a thief might try to pass a counterfeit coin, a word that fell from his mouth with a hollow ring.

Okay, okay, she thought.

I've learned a little. I've made a minor breakthrough. To where exactly?

To the possibility that Anthea McNair did not take her own life. No, you're being farfetched. You're walking through castles built in the clouds, you're afloat on fantasies, kid. You've been sucked into this bizarre family with all its locked rooms for too long. A break, that's what you need, a few days in another town, a place removed from the nightmares.

"I have your word, Christy?" he asked.

She nodded. "My word."

He clasped her against him and she could feel his hands try to work inside her blouse, she could feel the pressure of his hardness against her thighs, and for a moment she wanted to yield to him—but then she stepped back, disentangling herself because it was still too soon to give herself over to the act of loving her own husband.

Too many things were unclear.

Too many things unsaid, unexplained.

Things that—for the sake of her life, her marriage—had to be clarified and made clean again.

Leon Coldwind had been disturbed ever since the visit of Mrs. Christine McNair, distressed by the obvious anxiety on the woman's face, and more than a little unhappy at the way she had introduced herself under pretenses that were plainly false. He did not doubt that she was a journalist on a newspaper; rather, he put no faith in the story that she wanted to interview a certain client of his. She had married into the McNair family and she had stumbled, if stumbled was the word, into a series of existential quandaries, none of which she had been able to clear up.

He sat alone in the restaurant where he dined every night, toyed with his food because he had nothing like his usual appetite. In fact, he had drunk a little too much red wine and his brain was beginning to spin. It wasn't a condition he enjoyed especially, as a man who favored sobriety. Alcohol tended to exaggerate certain guilt feelings he had about himself. At law school, for instance, his ambition had been to operate legal clinics for the poor—it was an ambition that had died somewhat abruptly when he had been tempted by the finances of private practice.

Feeling a trifle maudlin, he cast his mind back to Mrs. McNair again, filled with an overwhelming sense of sorrow for her. The McNair family was not the kind one would wish one's own daughter to marry into; certain family histories had about them a darkness upon which no light could ever be made to shine.

He poured some more wine.

He ignored the passing dessert trolley—the cream concoctions caused his stomach to revolt.

Such a pretty young woman, he thought.

Pretty and puzzled.

He wondered what he might do that could possibly help her.

An anonymous note perhaps. Would that help?

Certain skeletal facts delivered by an unknown benefactor?

SM, he thought. He picked up his wineglass again and noticed that his tiny hand was shaking and what he realized was that Leonora Huntington had suddenly entered his mind, that her entrance was frightening to him. I am a man of unfathomable weaknesses, he told himself. I cannot begin to plumb the depths of my own cowardice.

But there was danger. Dear God, there was danger all right.

As soon as anybody came even remotely close to the secret target of Leonora's life, there was danger. (And he had a passing memory of another Mrs. McNair, a certain Anthea, who had apparently—poor poor thing—been driven to wrist-slitting.)

What was a man to do?

He emptied the bottle into his glass. Christy McNair had plunged herself into a world of madness.

And yet it wasn't madness, not by Leonora's standards anyhow.

It wasn't madness at all—and even if one could so define it, any good lawyer would find all kinds of mitigating circumstances for it.

Mitigating circumstances. How he loathed the jargon that was a part of his stock in trade. He ran a fingertip around the rim of his glass, creating a humming noise that drew the attention of other diners, and then he pondered the courses of action that might be open to him. I know this family, he thought. I have always known this family. I have known the abysses and the chasms.

He hesitated for a time, unsure of himself, and then had a waiter bring him a telephone. He called Information and was given the number of the McNair house in Bristol, Connecticut. He punched out the number. The phone rang for a long time without being answered. He put the receiver back, wondered if it was too late in his life to give way to a human impulse, then—more than a little encouraged by the wine—he dialed Leonora Huntington's number. When she answered he wanted to hang up, because the same old fear rushed through him with the sureness of an arrow. But he swallowed hard and gathered what little courage he possessed and he said, "Mrs. Huntington? This is Leon Coldwind."

"Why are you calling me at this hour?"

"It's about Mrs. McNair—"

"I'm sure it can wait until tomorrow—"

"No," he said. "It has to be now." Tomorrow, I won't be able to make such a telephone call.

"What exactly is on your mind?"

"Mrs. McNair—" He paused because he had the sudden feeling that he was dreaming, that he'd wake at any moment in a cold sweat.

"What about her?"

"I think . . . I think she deserves to know the truth."

"My dear Leon, have you been drinking?"

"A little wine—"

"May I suggest you cover your head with your bedsheets and sleep off this nonsense?"

"She's a young woman, she's pretty, she deserves—"

"She deserves nothing."

Coldwind eyed his empty wine bottle despairingly. One more glass, one more little glass and he could tell this woman what he really thought of her. But there wasn't even a dreg left in the goddamn thing.

He felt suddenly adrift, lost in a sea of his own making. Like a man drowning, going down for the third and final time. He moved his hand across the table and realized he had knocked over his empty wineglass. An embarrassment;

several waiters made a fuss over the single blood-colored stain on the linen.

"I have looked after your family business for a long time, Mrs. Huntington. I have protected your family name—"

"And?"

"I don't know how much longer I can do so—"

"Are we having a minor attack of conscience here?"

Confused, thirsty, dying for a fresh drink, Coldwind felt all his energies leave him. God, how he wished he had never made this call. What foolishness had possessed him? He could picture the fierceness of Leonora's beauty all at once and he was stunned. Am I really talking this way to her? Am I really being this stupid?

He wanted to apologize, to make amends, wanted to turn back the clock to that point where he had first dialed her number.

"You may feel better in the morning when you sober up," she said.

"Yes," he whispered. "Yes, yes, you're right, you're absolutely right, I'm not sure what got into me—"

"Wine." And then the line was dead, a taunting purr in his ear. He set the receiver down.

He covered his face with his hands and he thought: death and madness.

And a pretty young woman swinging on a trapeze whose support ropes would snap anytime Leonora chose to apply her knife to them.

He ordered a fresh drink and drank it down quickly before he hurried out into the night, where he might lose both himself and his nagging conscience.

Where he might finally come to terms with the fact that he was in no sense a hero.

* * *

Leonora pressed the power button for the window of the Cadillac and let the brisk night air blow against her face, stirring the thin dark veil she wore against her skin. She watched the hazy lights of Bristol come into sight, saw the faint orange-tinted smoke rise over the squalid industrial estates that lay on the outskirts of town. Bristol had never been her idea of urban perfection.

She instructed her driver to drop her in front of the Concorde and she forced herself inside, hating the sensation of being trapped, however briefly, in the revolving glass doors. She walked through the lobby, aware of people turning to look at her, but tonight she had no time to bask in this appreciation of her appearance. She stepped through the doorway that led to the bar, where Richard was already waiting for her at a table in the corner. She had rarely seen him look quite this good; he seemed to create a glow in the dim corner where he sat, an aura of physical perfection.

She smiled and sat down beside him, removing her black gloves and looking around for a waiter.

"I took the liberty of ordering you a drink," he said.

"Considerate of you, Richard"—and she folded her gloves very neatly and placed them on the table. A waiter materialized discreetly, just the way Leonora liked them to appear, with neither fuss nor ineptitude, and placed a glass of Scotch in front of her. She sipped it and she said, "You're looking extremely handsome, my dear. But you always were the most beautiful one in our family, weren't you?"

Richard appeared to accept this compliment casually. He pressed the tips of his long fingers together and studied his sister a moment. Then he said, "I talked to him."

"And how did he react?" she asked.

"He believed me."

Foolish Richard: he always assumed that the sincerity of his delivery convinced everybody. It may have fooled hundreds of women—those silly vain creatures, usually wealthy, with whom he had brief affairs in various cities— but there were other people who were not so easily taken in. "I am not so sure," she said. "I am not so sure that Zachary has believed you, my dear. I sometimes think that his love for this woman has quite blinded him." And she thought suddenly about Coldwind, Coldwind who had obviously gotten himself drunk to the point of bluster, a counterfeit bravery. Well, she had no intention of worrying about the little lawyer right now. She sipped a little more of her drink and examined her brother's face and wondered how it was that such beauty could conceal a rather dull intellect. But he had always been less smart than Zachary. Less smart, less stubborn, easier to control. Certainly she had managed for a long time to control them both, but there was a strength in Zachary that was harder to overcome. And she wondered if it were perhaps this quality, which she so disliked, that was nevertheless the thing that had always made him her favorite.

"I think he did believe me, Leonora," he said. "I could tell from the expression on his face. I don't think we need to worry about that marriage anymore."

"I have to disagree with you. I think our worries are only increasing. Consider this: Zachary confronts her about her supposed infidelities with you. She only has to deny it and poor Zachary tumbles into love all over again and forgets everything you ever told him." She paused; there was a smudge of lipstick on the rim of her glass. She wiped it off with a fingertip. "No, Richard, I believe the marriage is still far from being ruined. And you know what that means, don't you?"

He was shaking his head from side to side.

"Are you saying no to me, Richard?"

"Jesus Christ"—and he stared into his rum and Coke—"I don't want to go through it all again, Leonora. Please. Please don't make me."

"How could I ever make you do anything you didn't want to do?"

He looked down at the surface of the table as Leonora ran her fingertips up beneath the cuff of his sleeve, feeling his flesh tremble—and suddenly it was as if he were a child again, and she was touching him, making him feel secure and loved even after those bad times of pain when he would cry out aloud and there would be blood flowing, and thin trickles of vomit streaking the pillow beneath his face, those bad times when the rope burns on his wrists and thin ankles were more than he could bear, those terrible times when all he needed was a place away from the torture, the pain, where she might replace the bad memories with good feelings. And she could hear the door of the old trailer squeak open and the sound of heavy footsteps come crashing into the dark and the noise of the man stumbling against things—and they'd wait, shivering in the dark, to see who might randomly be chosen. . . .

"Anthea," she said.

Richard nodded.

"Anthea was being drawn into our world, Richard."

"Yes—"

"And Christy is closer still. But nobody must come near us, my dear, must they?"

"Nobody," he said. "Zachary's pain won't last forever, will it?"

"He'll get over Christy, don't you see? Don't you see how it protects you and me and Zachary as well?"

Richard was silent. Somebody was playing a piano across the room, a young girl with a tuneless voice who was murdering "Moonlight in Vermont."

Then he said, "She had to die, didn't she?"

"Anthea? Why, of course. Of course she had to die. You don't believe otherwise, do you?"

"No . . ."

"She went inside the bathtub, you remember that? She went inside the bathtub and she slit her wrists, the stupid woman. And Christy will probably do the same thing."

Richard nodded. "I want to get away from here, Leonora. I need to get out of this city. I can't take much more of it."

"I know that, my darling. Soon. Maybe tomorrow, the day after. But very soon."

"You promise?"

"Don't I always keep my promises?" But she'd never let him leave. Never.

"Yes." He nodded.

Leonora was quiet; she was filled with a sudden huge love for Richard, a love that was overflowing inside her, part devotion, part pity, a feeling too complex to break down into its composite parts. Love and loving—the most profound, the most magnificent of human qualities. And all at once, as if she were skimming old snapshots or running a slow-motion home movie through her brain, she could see Richard and Zachary as very small children—

then it all went wrong again

all wrong

all wrong the thoughts of murder

wrong wrong wrong

"Just remember, my dear," she said. "This love of Zachary's is a very dangerous thing."

She finished her drink and stood up and smiled at her brother for a moment.

A very dangerous thing, she thought.

The voice that came over the telephone at midnight was drunk to the point of complete incoherence, a babbling voice drowned every so often by the roar of passing traffic—and it took Christy several minutes, during which time she was on the point of hanging up at least three or four times, to realize she was listening to Coldwind, listening to his wild slur, his ranting. He muttered for a while about the nature of his oaths, his confidentiality, his duty—pronouncing the word as though it were the secret name of some forgotten god.

She was in the kitchen. She could hear Zachary move around at the top of the stairs and she thought: He imagines it might be his brother, that's what he's thinking, that's what he's still thinking, even now. Let him, she told herself. Let him believe what he likes because I've worked hard enough to convince him otherwise.

Now she tried to make out the lawyer's statements.

"I hate phone booths," he seemed to be saying. "I hate them. I hate the way everybody can just look inside and when they want you to get off the phone they rap on the glass with their goddamn nickels. . . . You know what I mean?"

"You're drunk, Mr. Coldwind."

"I should have been drunk a long time ago, dear lady. I should have drowned my shriveled old soul in alcohol before this."

There was a roaring on the line, maybe a passing truck. And the lawyer's voice was lost to her for a second.

". . . I love her, you see, you think I'm a little crazy, I love Leonora Huntington, at least I think I do although I shouldn't be saying these things to you, should I?"

"It's okay," Christy said, wondering what the real nature of this call might be, wondering what it was that had made Leon Coldwind drink to this extent.

"Lemme get to the point, my dear woman. Lemme show you this other side of me, show you I am not a coldhearted man, despite the frigid sound of my name."—and he laughed until she thought he was going to make himself sick. "The point is . . . I can't tell you very much about what you want to know, you understand me?"

"I understand."

"By God, you're an understanding lady, a fine lady . . . You might have married into a weird family, but you're a fine lady. Are you still listening to me, Mrs. McNair?"

"I'm listening, Mr. Coldwind."

"Leon. Please. Leon. Though I prefer Leo. Like the lion, huh?"

"Like the lion," she said.

"Anyway, you wanted to know about SM, right? Isn't that what you needed to know? The identity of SM."

"Yes—"

A silence and then more passing traffic whining across the distance.

"SM—these are the initials of Samuel McNair."

"Samuel McNair? Who's he?"

"Okay, now listen, you didn't learn any of this from me, I'm just an old hack of a lawyer, fine lady, but Samuel

McNair was the name of the father. The father of Leonora. Of Zachary. Of Richard. Old Sammy McNair. And you didn't hear it from good old discreet Coldwind, did you?"

Samuel McNair, she thought. Another name, a new name.

"Why are you telling me this?"

"Because guilt and a tapeworm are the same thing, dear woman. They both devour you eventually."

"And he did the paintings? Carved the statues?"

"He did the paintings. He carved the statues. And that's all I can tell you. Even a guilt-ridden old lawyer can only come out with so much, right? He's got to keep something heavy hanging on his conscience—otherwise why bother to practice law anyhow?"

And then Coldwind hung up. As he did so, Christy could hear the click of the upstairs extension and realized that Zachary must have been listening to the whole conversation.

She stood in the silent kitchen, motionless, wondering what else Zachary might be keeping back from her, how much more information he had failed to impart.

And wondering too why she kept feeling, in some far-off corner of her mind, a sense of terrible danger.

Richie listened to the sound of his own nightmare, to the way it screeched inside his head, feeling rough hands grip his body and turn him over on a narrow bed, feeling the way his blood dripped and hearing the screams of other children coming to him from a great distance, and then there was a weight pressed down on him, shoving him into the hard mattress, stifling him, crushing him, and he was sobbing with the awful pain of it all, sobbing in the darkness and

213

listening to the violent squeak of bedsprings and then it was over and there was the terrible emptiness in the aftermath of savagery—

A nightmare.

But he wasn't asleep.

He was sitting alone in the cocktail lounge of the Concorde Hotel, listening to a woman playing a piano.

He wasn't asleep at all.

He stood up, looked at the empty glasses on the table, and moved toward the lobby.

The death of Christy McNair.

Maybe that prospect was what had triggered the nightmare.

Maybe that was it.

And he stepped out of the lounge, unaware of the other patrons who were watching him.

Watching the man who had been sitting alone at a table and talking meaninglessly to himself.

14

Zachary woke where he'd fallen asleep on the sofa in the study. He looked blearily out into the darkness. A voice on a telephone, he thought, a man's voice mentioning a name, and the name had gone through his mind with the force of thunder.

It was the same thunder he heard right now, rolling around and around inside his brain.

Samuel McNair—the name came out of the recesses and folds of his memory like something erupting from the hot center of the earth.

Samuel McNair.

A memory of a monster.

A memory of death.

And suddenly he hated this house, he hated the way it felt, like some elaborate cage in which he was forever trapped, just as he felt ensnared by the past. There was a time to end it all, a time to say enough to things, a time to crack open surfaces and bring out the ghosts.

He was afraid now.

Afraid for himself, for Christy.

And for the thing he knew he had to do.

But if he didn't do it, if he didn't go through with it, then he knew that the rest of his life would be one of incarceration, of endless deceit.

Samuel McNair.

He would have rotted to nothing by this time.

Morning, the full flare of autumn, the sun gold and rich, as if it were a coin too splendid to spend. You wake on such mornings and life has a feeling to it of impossible wealth. Christy stretched, realized that Zachary had gone—taking with him to Manhattan not only his briefcase but his half-truths as well—and she sat up and glanced at the yellow window.

And then a memory, a fragment, of Leon Coldwind making a drunken call in the late hours of the night, an enigmatic explanation about the identity of the person known as SM, came back with all the texture of an ancient dream.

She got out of bed, stretched again, recalling how Zachary had been listening last night on the extension. A tiny trespass, an eavesdropping that had been a willful intrusion on her privacy—as if, despite anything they might have said to each other, he was still hiding things.

If Samuel McNair, if Zachary's own father had been the person who had painted the canvases, why had Zachary refused to remember it? She walked to the dressing-table mirror and looked at her uncombed hair and she wondered why love entailed so many lies.

What had been the nature of the relationship between Zachary and his father in any case? The tortuous complexities of family—and she remembered her own, remembered how simple her own had really been: a family life of straight lines, no crooked angles, no weird emotional geometry.

She considered the true nature of lies a moment. She considered the seeping poison that coursed through the blood. And what was worse was this—a point was reached where one could not distinguish between what was false and what true, as if every statement contained the seeds of its own contradiction.

When she finished dressing she went downstairs and made coffee in the kitchen. Halfway through her first cup, the telephone rang.

It was Leon Coldwind, sounding both sober and hungover.

And apologetic.

"I'm sorry I called you last night," he said. "I was hardly in a position to speak coherently and anything I might have said should be dismissed from your mind."

"You mentioned a certain Samuel McNair," she said, as if to jolt his memory.

"Did I? I'm sorry. I can't recall it now. The name means nothing to me."

"It meant something last night, Mr. Coldwind."

"Whatever it might have meant, I implore you to forget it now, Mrs. McNair. Indeed, I implore you to forget any questions you might have concerning the McNair family. All of them. I hope I make myself clear to you."

"You're telling me you've gone back to being a lawyer, is that it, Mr. Coldwind? You've gone back to hide behind your stuffy books and your briefs and all the rest of it—"

"In a manner of speaking." He was quiet for a time. Then, "I would especially ask you not to mention our little conversation to Leonora."

"She scares you, doesn't she? Why does she scare you so badly?"

There was no answer. And then Leon Coldwind said, "You'll have to excuse me if I terminate our conversation now. I have an incoming call on another line. Good-bye, Mrs. McNair. And good luck."

And good luck, she thought.

Good luck—as if he'd really meant it.

Samuel McNair, she thought again: what had happened to the man? Was he dead the way Coldwind had initially claimed? Or was he still alive somewhere?

She carried her coffee cup to the kitchen window and she looked out. There were two cars parked in the driveway, hers and Zachary's. How had he managed to get to the station this morning? Had he taken a cab? She gazed across the lawn toward the stand of trees in the distance.

Somebody was moving out there.

Somebody was moving between the trees.

She studied the figure for a time, thinking—with a cold sensation around her heart—that perhaps it was Richie. But then the figure disappeared down a slope and out of her sight.

She pressed her face against the glass, blinded a little by the full morning sunlight. Who the hell was out there?

She threw on her jacket and strode out across the lawn.

Halfway to the trees, she paused.

There was a sound of some kind, a faintly metallic sound that at first she couldn't recognize, couldn't quite place.

Then she started to walk again, feeling a movement of fear in her heart, a chill that the warmth of the sun did not dispel.

* * *

Leonora sat in the window seat and looked across the room, thinking she heard a sound on the landing outside, imagining it might be Daniel come to check on her—but she didn't need to see Daniel now.

She folded her hands in her lap and closed her eyes and rocked her body slightly back and forth. I have set the thing in motion, she thought. I have set the final chain of events in motion and suddenly, out of nowhere—as if matches were being lit along the fragile endings of her nerves—she felt pain.

But all the pains were old now.

There were no new ones lying ahead for any of them.

She opened her eyes and she thought about Richard.

What time was it? she wondered.

She wasn't wearing a watch and the realization that she didn't have any idea of time filled her with panic.

She turned and looked out of the window across the grounds, trying to assess the time from the position of the sun. Ten? Eleven? She wasn't sure. Far below, she could see Daniel Huntington snoozing in a deck chair, a pale blue hat pulled down across his eyes. Then it had to be somewhere between ten and eleven because that was when he had his morning nap, which meant—

Which meant that Richard would have started out already.

Zachary would be in Manhattan and his wife would be all alone.

And that would be the end of it.

That would be the last of the threats.

This realization uplifted her.

She would move back into the old house with Zachary and Richard as well and then everything would begin to feel

219

normal. Looking after Zachary, taking care of poor Richard, just the pleasure of those things.

The two children together again under her care.

And Zachary's lovely little wife dead.

Christy reached the trees, where she stopped; a large dark bird flew out of the branches overhead, wings flapping, huge claws glistening in the sunlight. She watched it go; then she realized that the sound she'd been listening to had stopped some moments before. She looked this way and that, saw how the trees fell away with the slope of the land, saw how the sun burnished the fading leaves. That sound— why wasn't she able to place it? Why? Familiar and yet not. Now there were only silences, an absence of songbirds, as if the world were suddenly empty, devoid of all life.

Then she was walking down the slope of land, feeling brittle leaves crack underfoot, hearing wood snap.

And there it was again.

That same metallic sound; metal, hard metal striking something soft.

Striking the soft earth.

A spade, she thought.

That was the noise she heard.

Somebody was out there, masked by the trees, digging a hole.

She went forward a little way and felt something hard strike her foot. When she looked down she saw a twisted piece of rusted mesh, such as might have been part of a screen door long ago.

She skirted around it, following the sound again.

Then she stopped.

She stopped, stared through the trees, saw Zachary

plunging a large spade into the earth, plunging with a frenzy, shoulders rising and falling, arm muscles straining.

Why? Why is he doing this?

She called out his name but he didn't hear her, didn't turn to look.

She went closer until she was only a few yards away from him and she said his name a second time but again he paid no attention to her.

"Zachary."

And for one frozen moment, for an arctic second of her life, she had the feeling that he was digging a grave.

A grave for whom?

She leaned against the trunk of a tree and she asked herself the question again.

Something was spinning inside her, something turning over and over.

Zachary had twisted his face around to look at her.

The expression there.

How could you read anything from such a blank expression?

He saw her, he didn't see her.

He doesn't seem to know me. He shows no sign of recognition.

And then he turned away from her again and the spade was rising and falling and the air was filled with soft earth, tufts of brown grass, the debris of tossed leaves.

"Zachary," she said. And she went closer still.

What is he looking for buried here in the earth?

And then she was standing directly behind him and she could hear the way he was grunting from exertion and she could smell the sweat that rose from his body and she had the feeling, the awful falling feeling, that he had gone away from her forever.

Dear Zachary. My love. My dear Zachary.

The metal of the spade glinted, the air was filled with dirt, tiny stones, pebbles, grass.

"Zachary," and she put out one hand to touch his shoulder, but he acted as if he felt absolutely nothing. She stared into the hole he was digging, watched the turning of surprised worms and the scurrying of panicked ants and the scuttling motions of earwigs—all the crawling things that lay just beneath the surface of the ground.

Please, Zachary, please, say something to me, tell me what it is you're doing here, just tell me.

He brushed her hand away and drove the head of the spade into the earth with his foot, turning more soil over, turning it as if it were the only thing in the world of which he was conscious.

Digging, digging, thrusting.

Is this place for me? she wondered. Is he digging this place for me?

She turned her face upward to the sun—masked by branches, half-hidden by the ruined leaves of the season— and she realized she wanted to run, she wanted to get away from this place, but somehow she couldn't bring herself to move, almost as if she were magnetized by the depth of the hole in front of her.

And then she saw it.

She heard the spade strike something hard and she saw a movement of something bleached, white, something bone-white to which dark soil was clinging.

"Zachary—"

He hammered the spade deeper now, thrusting with an

energy she'd never seen on his face before, his jaw tight and his mouth nothing more than a single determined line and his eyes glazed, and she stepped backward, stepped away, gasping as the head of the spade raised a skull out of the grave, a skull in which there was a long narrow crack.

This hollow grinning skull, this thing that had once been human.

And still he wouldn't stop digging, unearthing a rib cage, more bones, brittle skinny fingers, and then she was trying to haul him away from the edge of the grave but he pushed her aside and—raising the shovel as if it were a weapon—brought it down again and again on the skeleton, smashing the metal head against rib bones, against the skull, hammering and hammering until he sank to his knees in exhaustion at the side of the hole and was crying quietly, tears running down his cheeks, his mouth distended in a pain that was beyond articulation.

She knelt beside him, one hand resting against his trembling arm.

He turned his face to her and his mouth hung open and although he was trying to say something no words came out of him. Only a silence, a terrible silence.

And she wondered at the depths of his hatred, at the reaches of his violence. Just as she wondered how much it had cost him in sheer human effort to keep this skeleton buried far inside himself.

"Samuel McNair." His voice was a whisper.

She nodded. Samuel McNair.

"It was time." He buried his face into her shoulder and she held him for a long while.

"It was time," he said again. "And when I heard his name on the telephone last night, I knew it."

223

She ran her fingers through his hair and tried to soothe him but he wouldn't stop trembling, he just wouldn't stop. She looked toward the pit he'd dug, she looked at the pale bones, and for the first time she had an insight into a secret history, a fragmented perception of a past that had always haunted Zachary.

"We killed him," he said. "We killed him. Leonora. Richard. Myself. We murdered him and we buried his body here."

And you, Zachary, she thought, you have been the caretaker of this dead place.

Until this moment.

She rose unsteadily to her feet.

She turned her face away from the sight of the skeleton.

No, she thought. The puzzles are not over yet.

He saw her Jaguar come hurrying out of the driveway and he swung his car around immediately, settling into the traffic lane just behind her, wondering where she was going in such a rush. She was supposed to be home alone today. She was supposed to be home.

Today was supposed to be the day of her suicide.

Daniel Huntington had been dreaming about himself as a young man; he was wearing a panama hat and a white suit and strolling along a promenade somewhere, possibly in the south of France, although, given the nature of dreams, he could not be absolutely certain. What aroused him from his dreaming was the noise of a car coming up the driveway. He opened his eyes, blinked, saw the wine-colored car come to a halt outside the house and a young woman get out and slam the door shut. He rose shakily from his deck chair and hurried across the lawn to speak to her but she was agile, quick, going up the steps to the front door before he could catch her.

"Mrs. McNair!"

She turned when she heard his voice. Then she was ringing the doorbell as if quite unconscious of his existence.

"Mrs. McNair," he said, and he caught her by the arm. "Where are you going?"

"I've come to see Leonora," she answered, and he observed a look of such determination in her eyes that he was momentarily silenced.

"She doesn't want to see anybody, I'm afraid—"

"She'll see me," the young woman said.

"I hardly think so—"

But the door was being opened by Skyler and the young woman was already brushing past the butler and striding along the hallway. Daniel Huntington hurried after her, wheezing, trying to match her stride.

"Where is she?" she asked.

"I told you, she's busy, she doesn't want to be disturbed, don't you understand that?" Out of breath; he realized his voice carried no authority whatsoever.

"Is she upstairs?" the woman asked.

"I'll call the police," he said.

"I doubt it," and then she was climbing the stairs two at a time.

He thought: Leonora is in her private room, her private world. No one must disturb her.

But he could already hear Christy McNair opening and closing doors all the way above him—and suddenly he was filled with tension, his heart a tight, pounding muscle in the middle of his chest.

"Mrs. McNair! Please!"

But she wasn't paying any attention, he could hear her rise ever further in the house, ignoring his shouts and cries. Higher and higher she was going—dear God, it would only be a matter of time before she found Leonora's room, it would only be a matter of time before the structure of everything gave way and the sounds of ruin filled the whole house. He reached the first landing, where he paused because his breathing was difficult and his limbs trembling.

And then he knew the woman had found Leonora's room because he could hear the door opening and closing and the surprised sound of his wife's voice. On the landing, motionless, afraid, sensing his world fragmenting around him, he waited.

"My dear, you are quite the last person I expected to see," Leonora said, rising from her seat at the window and smiling with a graciousness that Christy had not anticipated. She came forward, extending her hand, offering her cheek for a kiss that Christy would not give. "However, now that you are here, welcome to my little room."

Christy took her eyes away from the woman's face and looked around the white-walled room: what kind of place was this? What kind of little universe had Leonora fabricated for herself here? The tiny piles of kids' clothing, most of it old stuff. The pen-and-ink drawings on the walls, which depicted Zachary and Richard as very small boys. And along the shelves old toys, broken toys, soft toys bruised from too much handling—there was a whole world here that might have been created out of the things you would find in a thrift-store basement. But they hadn't been purchased from any such source, because Leonora, smiling and calm, was wandering through all this stuff and touching it lovingly, as if each item was invested with some special meaning only for her.

Christy shut her eyes, feeling a little dizzy.

Leonora was holding her by the elbow. When she opened her eyes she saw—pressed to the far wall—a couple of canvases, the canvases she should have expected, might have predicted, the same four figures shrouded in terror.

It's a museum here, she thought. It's a shrine to some unthinkable past. It's where Leonora preserves her history, her love, her warped, twisted love.

"Do you like my little room, Christy?" she asked.

Christy nodded.

"You don't need to patronize me, you know," Leonora said, the smile heavy with charm.

"I didn't intend to, Leonora," and Christy paused, thinking about Zachary digging deep into the soft earth. She moved toward the canvases at the back of the room. Four figures, always four. Leonora and Richie and Zachary—was the other one Samuel McNair? She turned around and looked at Leonora and she said, "We found the grave. Zachary found it this morning."

"Ah, Zachary. I've always considered Zachary the one most likely to betray family bonds. I loved him, of course, and I still love him with all my heart, but he forgets his ties, he thinks he can live without them." Leonora moved toward the window seat and sat down, clasping her hands. "I always knew that he'd be the one to dig up the past. Dear God, I tried. I truly tried to make him aware of his blood bond, his responsibilities to our little family. I imagine I failed in that respect."

"Failed? Failed how?"

227

Leonora looked faintly mysterious. "It's always a problem to hold a family together, Christy. There are always so many external threats. Like wives, for example—"

"Like Anthea, you mean. Like me."

"Precisely. But only because there are certain things you could never understand, nor could you ever be expected to understand. You were not of the blood, a fact for which you can hardly be blamed, my dear."

Where? Christy wondered. Where in the name of God is this going?

"I raised those two boys, Christy. I raised them with as much love as any mother might show her children, perhaps even more. I raised them because there was nobody else to do it—"

"What about their father?" Christy asked.

Leonora rose, looking suddenly solemn, moving around the room, moving through all the broken treasures of her past. "I want to tell you something you may have some difficulty in believing, my dear. There are certain people in this world to whom cruelty is perfectly natural, as natural as breathing. Shall we say that they lack something in humanity, as if they were born without a certain quality, a compassion, if you will?"

Compassion, Christy thought.

What kind of compassion was it that drove Anthea to her death? What would you call that, Leonora?

"Our father was one such creature." And here Leonora paused, as if she were on the edge of a memory too terrible to mention. "He was one such creature . . ."

Christy could feel the tension rise inside her, run around the rim of her heart. A man dies, no, three children murder him and bury him, and Zachary becomes the caretaker of the place of death.

"Picture this, if you will, my dear. Picture three children subjected to the kinds of cruelty that defy the imagination—" She hesitated again and for a moment Christy felt an awful pity for this woman. "In those days, there was a trailer parked in the grounds of the house where you and Zachary live. It was one of those primitive aluminum things, kept locked day and night. In winters, it was unheated. In summers, it was not cooled. It was, in effect, a prison for three young children. That, you would think, is bad enough, no?"

"Yes," Christy said, and waited, even if she didn't want to hear any more.

"The man was a monster. An indisputable fact. However . . ."

Another pause now; Leonora picked up a stuffed toy, a decrepit bear, and stroked it gently with her fingers. "However, he would come on certain nights, this father of ours, and he would routinely torture his children. He would routinely take me. I am talking about small children, remember. I was thirteen. Zachary was six. Richard was eight. It became an everyday occurrence in our world, Christy. We began to expect it because we were always rewarded with food. First the pain, then the food. A system of punishments and rewards. And when he had to go away anywhere for a day or so, he would bind the three of us together with a short chain. And if by any chance he heard us crying—out of hunger, out of pain—he would inflict certain tortures on us. I will not go into any detailed description of these—it would be enough to say that I have never been able to conceive a child as a consequence of our father's actions. Is that clear enough for you?" Leonora smiled horribly. "I think he was unhinged by the death of his wife when she was giving birth to Zachary. I rather think he blamed all the children for that."

Christy leaned against the wall. It crossed her mind that perhaps all she was listening to were more lies, more fabrications—how could she know now? How could she tell? There had been so many.

"Rape. Hunger. Cold. The intense heat of summer. We were subjected to all manner of things. And so—" Leonora stopped now, smiling at Christy in her way.

"When I was fourteen years of age I smashed his skull in with a hammer. He was drunk, he had Zachary's hands tied behind his back, he was pulling the kid's clothes from his body, and—and it was simply one of those moments when one understands that a situation has to stop, that it cannot go any further; a limit has been reached and passed. The three of us dragged the body out of the trailer and we buried it.

"And so I raised them, I raised them with the kind of love they had never known in their short and miserable lives, and I raised them with the knowledge of the terrible bond that existed between us. The terrible secret we might never share with anybody outside this small circle of three. Do you understand what I did? Do you understand the kind of love I gave them? Do you realize how hard it has been to hold our blood together? I doubt that you do, Christy. Like Anthea, like Daniel Huntington, you are just another outsider trying to belong to a group that cannot tolerate outsiders. It is as simple as that, my dear. It is quite that simple. And I cannot buy you off the way I can that little whore Coldwind—"

Christy was thinking now of Anthea. She swung her face around and looked at Leonora.

"What kind of threat could somebody like Anthea pose, for God's sake?"

Leonora shook her head. "Who knows? There was always the possibility of discovery, my dear. She had to die and it had to look like a suicide. Nobody enters the circle. And poor Zachary—well, Zachary thinks he can be free of the past, he thinks he can live out his own life."

It had to look like a suicide—

It had to look like a suicide—

Anthea . . .

"Zachary should never have married. He broke our rules by doing so. Not once, but twice. We are a small group of people shuttered by our own past deeds. The only reason I ever married was to provide for Richard. Courtesy of Daniel Huntington, I make him a generous allowance—on the understanding that he does not take the same path as Zachary."

"And so Anthea died, but not by her own hand."

"As you say, my dear."

"And does Zachary know how she died?"

"It was such an obvious suicide, wasn't it?"

A young woman is held down in a bathtub and a razor blade is taken and sliced through her wrists and all the world thinks: Poor thing, poor depressed thing, unrequited love was too much for her.

And now something similar is planned for me, she thought, something along those same lines, a fate like Anthea's—and all because Leonora lived in the perpetual fear of her sacred blood secrets being decoded by strangers, lived in fear of an old murder coming to light, lived in terror of retribution. How had Zachary lived with the same terror all those years? And she could see it now, she could see the nature of the conspiracy between Leonora and Richie, she could see how they would leave nothing to chance because Zachary was the weak link, that part of the whole chain which lacked their awful integrity.

Zachary, who had dug up the corpse as if he were finally exorcising ancient demons.

And now—what was going to happen to her?

Think, she told herself. Think hard.

And she walked to the far wall and looked at the canvases and tried to force her mind into some feeble form of action.

Leonora, watching her, said, "Of course, I was able to generate a certain amount of income from the sales of those paintings. Never enough, naturally. Never enough to support dear Richard." She paused and looked directly at Christy, smiling again. "Those boys have been my whole life. I doubt if you could ever understand a love that grew in conditions of impossible adversity, Christy. I doubt if you could ever know that feeling."

I don't know if I want to, Christy thought. She stared at Leonora, more afraid than she had ever been in her life.

"Why are there four figures?" she asked. Ask anything. Just win time to think.

"Samuel McNair had a particularly dark view of the world. He saw himself and his children as something from a nightmare. He saw the entire world as a nightmare. . . . There was nothing he did not despise. And there was nothing that did not terrify him, my dear."

Silence, silence in the room, a silence that beat against the walls.

Christy listened to this without really hearing it. All she knew now was that she had to get out of this room, she had to get away, home to Zachary to find that he had—once and for all—demolished all the dark blemishes of the past. She wanted to find out that he was finally free from all the constraints, all the imprisonments, that Leonora, in the full madness of her love, had imposed upon him. She glanced at the pictures again and all she could think about was the insanity of this bloodline, this pact created so long ago that it should have been allowed to slip, finally and quietly, into oblivion.

"Now you know," Leonora said. "Now you know it all."

Why did that sound so menacing? Christy wondered. So threatening, so final? I know it all because I am expendable.

"I take it you have plans for me, Leonora," she said.

Leonora shook her head. "There's the door, Christy. Go ahead. Open it. Go down the stairs. Walk away."

"And then what?"

Leonora shrugged. "Some secrets are carried to the grave, my dear. I find a lovely pattern in that, don't you?"

Christy turned, walked to the door, opened it tentatively, stepped out onto the landing. They killed Anthea, she thought. They will also kill me.

And she reached the stairs.

As she did so, she realized that somebody was coming up toward her, a figure rising slowly through the thin light.

Her own sense of fear seemed to her just then a thing of geometrical perfection, as if all the other sensations she'd experienced in her lifetime had been distorted and ill-formed.

She clutched the rail, looking down.

Looking down at Richie coming up toward her.

Richie, who had not been able to ruin her marriage by

233

inducing her into infidelity, but who was determined now to ruin it with her death.

And when she turned her face to look back up the stairs, she saw Leonora smiling, looking down at her, her expression one of curious indifference, as if she no longer cared one way or another about Christy's fate.

15

The skull. It was strange how little a skull resembled anything lifelike, as if the casting off of skin had reduced the structure to an artifact that might have been made by an ancient craftsman. Now one could no longer imagine it coated with skin, could no longer imagine lips, eyes in the sockets, a tongue creating comprehensible language. And when Zachary had dug it up, had violated the grave with such relentless energy, it was as if a tense spring far inside him had suddenly slackened, as if he had come to understand the nature of liberty.

Samuel McNair. A forgotten name.

Forgotten, repressed, until he had heard it last night on the telephone when he'd been listening to Christy's conversation with Leon Coldwind——and years, like the shed skins of reptiles, had fallen away from him, and all the pains Samuel McNair had inflicted upon him vanished to a point where he could no longer remember them.

Samuel McNair, about whom he had once felt guilty.

Whose death he had once regretted.

He had dropped the skull back into the soil, kicked soft

235

earth over it with his foot. Then he had turned and walked back toward the house in time to see Christy's car go screaming out of the driveway—puzzling him, snapping him back into the present, as if he were suddenly emerging from an old mist. He'd watched the car go, then he'd looked toward the facade of the house, really seeing it for the first time.

One of us must go on living here, Leonora had said.

One of us must stand guard over the past.

It should be you, Zachary.

It always has been you, Zachary. You were the keeper of a sacred flame that burned only in the mind of Leonora and nowhere else.

A flame that had simply spluttered out, leaving your nostrils filled with the smell of old, burning wax.

. Leaving you with the absence of Christy.

Where had she gone anyhow?

The first thought that came to his mind was that she'd driven to the police, she'd gone to the police with the information about the grave—and he was afraid again, he was scared almost as if he'd never experienced his brief moment of freedom at all. Scared of Leonora, of what Leonora would do when she found out that he'd opened the grave, of what she might do to punish him. Dear Christ, why did his emotions always return like some restless tide to the idea of Leonora? Why was she always the center of his gravity?

He paced the room. What to do? What was he going to do?

You have to confess to Leonora. You're like a little kid again carrying all your troubles and woes to her, waiting for either the rush of her anger or the touch of her love.

236

No, he thought.

Goddammit, no, he was sick of his own fear, tired of his own cowardice, weary of having Leonora dictate his life to him—

You stand by yourself.

You love Christy and you have to stand by yourself.

There is nothing to beg for, there is no forgiveness to crave.

You are not an addict to the past.

There's Christy, and Christy is life, Christy is future—

Leonora is just the sick, dead past, the cloisters of useless memory—

And he turned and left the house, rushing down the steps to his car, realizing that his freedom from the past had been more than a heightened illusion, more than a tiny dream of bravery.

Christy backed into the room, Richie watching her. She was aware of Leonora standing immediately behind her, filling the space between herself and the window as if she meant to block all light from reaching Christy. Richie was smiling, his hands hanging at his sides, his expression strangely dreamlike—she was afraid of this man crossing the floor toward her.

A way out, she thought.

Where was the way out of this?

She clenched her hands, as if she meant to fight, but she didn't have any strength in her body. She just kept backing away, backing until she could go no further, because Leonora was standing immediately behind her, her hands softly massaging Christy's shoulders. Massaging, caressing, as if it was love and not death that was the issue here.

They mean to kill me. The way Anthea was killed. They mean to kill me in such a way that it will be just another suicide—

She glanced at Leonora. That smile. That terrible smile. How could a face so beautiful wear such an ugly smile?

And something glinted in Richie's hand, something metallic and awful, sharp in the savage sunlight that strafed the room. Sharp, dreadful, the killing edge. She thought a second, a brittle second, about Anthea's papers—

the real . . . comes from L

The real fear.
The real force.
They were both applicable. Both the same.

She looked at Richie, her vision clear, and she understood that he was carrying an old-fashioned razor in his hand. Maybe it was the same blade that had opened Anthea's veins, the same vicious edge of cutting steel.

She tried to free herself from Leonora's grasp, tried to twist away, make it to the other side of the room, somehow make it past the obstacle of Richie (how? how? how?), but Leonora was strong, unexpectedly strong, her hands gripping like claws—

Then Leonora said. "Kill her, Richard. Kill her."

How long would it take him to get to Leonora's house if he hurried?

Twenty, thirty minutes? He got into his car and drove quickly down the driveway and onto the street. And then his mind was horribly blank, he couldn't recall where Leonora lived. A place that begins with the letter C. Something like

238

Crestford, Crestingham, Jesus Christ, why couldn't he remember?

Why couldn't he force his stalled mind into action?

He hit the freeway, staring at road signs, looking for anything that might be remotely familiar, but the blankness that was creeping through his mind had turned to a kind of uncomprehending numbness and he couldn't find his way through the fog of his own brain.

As he drove he realized his hands ached from handling the spade.

CrestSomething.

But Crest what?

And then he saw the freeway sign, he saw the name CRESTWICH; it was ten miles away.

Ten miles.

Okay. Ten miles.

And then traffic lights. Stop signs. Schoolkids being led across the street by a crossing guard, so many kids. When they'd passed he hit the gas hard again and he didn't let up until he reached Crestwich—

And he thought: There's nothing more you can do to me, Leonora, there's nothing more I owe you, I have a life to lead—

Then he had to remember where her house was located and it took him ten minutes, ten unbearable minutes to find the place—

There it was.

The big house.

The big house that had always made him nervous.

And Christy's Jaguar parked out front.

Why the hell had she come here? Had she come to tell Leonora about the grave? Sweet Jesus—

He jumped out of the car and ran toward the doorway, passing the idiotic group of statues as one might try to bypass a particularly old nightmare, and then he was inside the house and moving down the hallway, where Daniel Huntington emerged from the gloom, an expression on his face that was sorrowful, weary.

"You're looking for them," he said. "I expect you're looking for your wife and Leonora," and he raised one finger, pointing to the stairs. "At the very top. God help you."

Zachary hesitated a moment and then he began to climb.

She felt she had no senses left, that she was deaf and blind and dumb, her nerve endings gone; she felt as if she'd stepped inside a world of indifference where nothing could possibly matter to her again.

It was the end of everything.

She watched Richie come closer, closer to her still.

She watched the blade glinting. She saw her own tiny reflection in the steel.

"Kill her, kill her, Richard," Leonora was saying, as if she were a cheerleader on the sidelines of some utterly grotesque game.

I die like this, Christy thought.

I die like a condemned animal—

Fight, she thought.

You could fight—

And she tried to claw out at Richie and the steel nicked her flesh and she saw her own blood rise from the surface of her broken skin, she saw Richie's face, beautiful and determined and murderous, she heard the sound of his breathing—

240

No no no.

This is not the real world, this is another place altogether, something I can escape from, something I can run from.

But there was no place to hide.

No place to go.

A crack in the door, a slight opening, and what he saw in the white-walled room beyond made him freeze, turned his flesh cold. He was thinking: Anthea; he was thinking about Anthea and Richard in bed together, he was remembering how he had peered through the opening of a bedroom door a long time ago and seen their bodies pressed together, and worse—Christ, the worst thing about the memory was the look on Anthea's face of ecstasy, something he'd never seen there before, and he remembered turning and crawling away, hiding somewhere in the darkness of the night. A worm. Nothing more than a goddamn worm.

He trembled.

He pushed the door open a little further.

He stepped inside the room.

Listened to the sound of his brother breathing hard. Saw the metal shine in his hand. Saw Christy's eyes shut tight, her mouth open, her fists clenched—

And on the other side of the room, like a spectator at some particularly obscene event, his sister.

His beloved Leonora.

Leonora and Richard. His flesh, his blood.

And here was Christy, here was his wife, his love, and what was happening to her was what had happened to Anthea before her and what would presumably happen to any other woman who ever came along and wanted to belong in his life.

Any other woman.

He didn't want any other woman.

Only Christy.

And he remembered the mad way he had been digging that morning, the craziness of his exertions, as if he were more than digging up some old skeleton, but burying something as well, burying a dead past and with it all the madness that had weakened him—

Christy cried out to him.

He thought: It doesn't matter that these people are my flesh and blood now.

Christy is more than that to me—

And he strode across the room, dragging Richard's body away, dragging him away across the floor and then turning to face Leonora.

"Zachary," she said. "How dare you come in here!"

He ignored her, ignored the sight of his brother sitting in the corner, and, reaching down, he held Christy to his body, feeling the way she trembled, tasting the salt of her tears against her cheeks.

Leonora moved forward. "Zachary, I warn you. I will not stand for this kind of behavior. I will not stand for it—"

He stood upright, watching her for a second.

And he clenched his hand, clenched it so tightly that the knuckles were bone-white, and then he stepped toward her, the fist raised in front of her face.

She smiled at him. "You wouldn't strike me, Zachary," she said.

A moment of confusion went through him. No, she was right, he wouldn't strike her. He wouldn't touch her. Others would take care of her soon enough. He put an arm around

Christy and led her slowly out of the room and onto the landing.

Leonora followed him, watching him take Christy down the stairs.

"You think this ends here, Zachary. You think you can forget all the things that hold us together. You imagine you are free, don't you?"

But he wasn't listening.

He wasn't listening to her words.

And he didn't listen to her laughter as he stepped out through the front door, his arm around Christy's waist, out into the burning sunshine.

ABOUT THE AUTHOR

THOMAS ALTMAN is a writer who lives in Arizona. His first novel for Bantam was the very successful *Kiss Daddy Goodbye*, published in 1980. It was followed by *The True Bride*, and then by *Black Christmas*. The next Thomas Altman novel is in the works.

BLACK CHRISTMAS
by Thomas Altman

Someone has a special gift for the young women of Murdock . . .

Christmas in Murdock. A time of cosy safety, snowy sidewalks, and carolling children. But this holiday season, someone is baiting Sheriff Dunsmore in a bizarre and deadly game.

Someone is stalking the young women he knows and loves . . . seducing them with icy steel . . . leaving them for him to find – far too late.

It's the night before Christmas. The frightened town edges toward panic. And Dunsmore is about to receive the most terrifying gift of all . . .

0 552 12472 9   £1.95

THE TRUE BRIDE
by Thomas Altman

Ellen Campbell and her husband, Eric, are cheerfully awaiting the birth of their first baby. She is happy; Eric is devoted to her, her friend Vicky is reliable and her mother had moved halfway across the country to be with her.

Then she notices things going wrong; little things at first, then much more frightening, like her blue shirt cut to shreds, the black car always following her, the telephone messages that make no sense. Soon, Ellen is so distracted by the terrible things happening to her that she fears for her life and that of her unborn child.

Set in the stifling heat of suburban Arizona, *The True Bride* is an intensely chilling and horrifying story of insanity, the ultimate marriage of love and terror.

'A well-done narrative of paranoia à la Rosemary's Baby'
Publishers Weekly

0 552 12232 7   £1.75

ALL FALL DOWN
by John Saul

A terrifying story that weaves medical fact with ingenious scientific speculation – a tale of fear . . .

Something is happening to the children of Eastbury, Massachusetts. Something nameless that causes healthy babies to turn cold in their cots. Something that touches every mother's secret fear that she may have passed on to her child some terrible, life-taking flaw.

A small town, a family in jeopardy, a sudden terror . . . Against this backdrop, John Saul has created a compelling, terrifying and chilling psychological thriller.

0 552 12298 X   £1.95

MINE TO KILL
by David St Clair

Best selling author of CHILD POSSESSED.

The true account of Canada's number one case of possession and exorcism.

On Wednesday, 28th August, 1878, Esther Cox, a plain, unassuming girl from the town of Amherst in Nova Scotia rode out in a buggy on her first date. Storm clouds lowered on the horizon; later there was lightning and torrential rain. Esther returned at nightfall, soaked through and too distraught to speak to her family: her innocent trip had turned into the beginning of a personal nightmare.

At first there were rustlings in her bedroom at night, then unseen hands gouged a terrible message on her wall:

ESTHER COX, YOU ARE MINE TO KILL!

On the third night, Esther leapt from her bed: 'Oh my God' she screamed 'I'm dying! Please dear God! I'm dying!'

This is the chilling story of a girl's possession by malevolent spirits. Like CHILD POSSESSED, everything in this book actually happened.

0 552 12587 3   £2.50

OTHER HORROR TITLES AVAILABLE
FROM CORGI/BANTAM

☐	12472 9	BLACK CHRISTMAS	Thomas Altman	£1.95
☐	12232 7	THE TRUE BRIDE	Thomas Altman	£1.75
☐	24010 2	KISS DADDY GOODBYE	Thomas Altman	£1.95
☐	09156 1	THE EXORCIST	William Peter Blatty	£1.95
☐	08272 4	PSYCHO	Robert Bloch	£1.50
☐	12186 X	PSYCHO 2	Robert Bloch	£1.75
☐	12691 8	WHAT ABOUT THE BABY?	Clare McNally	£1.75
☐	11132 5	CHILD POSSESSED	David St. Clair	£1.95
☐	12587 3	MINE TO KILL	David St. Clair	£2.50
☐	17171 2	BRAINCHILD	John Saul	£2.50
☐	12568 7	NATHANIEL	John Saul	£1.95
☐	12298 X	ALL FALL DOWN	John Saul	£1.95
☐	12125 8	THE HUNGER	Whitley Strieber	£1.75